Nerves tig̶͟͞ ̶͟͞ul ball inside ̶̶̶

His words created an image of long nights and the scent, texture and feel of his body beneath her hands, her mouth. The way he could drive her wild…dear heaven, beyond *wild*, with a lovemaking that broke all barriers. Fast and passionately *driven*, or long, tender and slow… he had the power to take her places she hadn't known existed. Sensual nirvana, in all its connotations.

She'd thought it was enough. More than enough. Nothing, she'd imagined, could touch them.

Now Lianne's chin lifted and her eyes seared his. 'I'm no longer *yours*.'

He was silent for what seemed an age, and his voice when he spoke was dangerously soft. 'No?'

Helen Bianchin was born in New Zealand and travelled to Australia before marrying her Italian-born husband. After three years they moved, returned to New Zealand with their daughter, had two sons, then resettled in Australia. Encouraged by friends to recount anecdotes of her years as a tobacco sharefarmer's wife living in an Italian community, Helen began setting words on paper and her first novel was published in 1975. An animal lover, she says her terrier and Persian cat regard her study as much theirs as hers.

Recent titles by the same author:

HIS PREGNANCY ULTIMATUM
THE SPANIARD'S BABY BARGAIN

THE DISOBEDIENT BRIDE

BY
HELEN BIANCHIN

MILLS & BOON®

First published in Great Britain 2005
Harlequin Mills & Boon Limited,
Eton House, 18-24 Paradise Road, Richmond, Surrey TW9 1SR

© Helen Bianchin 2005

ISBN 0 263 84136 7

Set in Times Roman 10½ on 12½ pt.
01-0405-38765

Printed and bound in Spain
by Litografia Rosés, S.A., Barcelona

CHAPTER ONE

LIANNE jabbed the call-button with unnecessary force, and bit down a husky oath as her fingernail split.

The day had barely begun and already it was shaping up to surpass Friday the thirteenth at its worst.

In the space of two hours she'd dealt with a flat tyre, had the ATM chew up her Access card, and misjudged a balancing act with her car keys and her cellphone in which the cellphone had lost, damaged beyond repair.

The lift whispered to a halt, the doors slid open and she stepped inside, silently willing the electronic cubicle a swift clear passage to the uppermost floor, housing the imposing legal offices of Sloane, Everton, Shell and Associates.

Make my day, she silently challenged and barely contained her frustration as the lift's ascent was punctuated by numerous stops...ten in all, a fact she knew because she counted each and every one of them.

The lift drew to a halt, the doors slid open and Lianne walked into the office lobby of one of the city's most prestigious legal firms.

There was late, and there was *late*, Lianne perceived as she crossed to Reception. A few minutes, even five over time was acceptable...thirty, however, was stretching things a bit far.

Two attractive young women manned Reception, alternating between the central phone console and tending the day's scheduled client appointments. Both were tall, one blonde, the other dark-haired, each resembling sleek models moonlighting as office assistants, and creating a complementary balance.

A deliberate choice, Lianne surmised, aware of Michael Sloane's predilection for *image*.

An explanation was in order, together with an apology, and Lianne offered the necessary words.

'Any messages?' She could do cool professionalism. She'd had considerable practice in donning the requisite façade.

'They're on your desk.' The blonde checked the appointment register. 'Pamela Whitcroft is waiting for you in the client lounge.'

Oh, my. Just what she needed. The social doyenne sought legal opinion on the most trivial matters, and delighted in consulting...*testing*, Pamela assured Michael, the expertise of each and every one of his qualified staff.

Lianne raised her eyes heavenward. *Why me?* At least, why me *today*?

'Give me five minutes, then send her in.' She turned and made her way along the curved corridor to her office where she took time to scan her messages, check Pamela's file, and spare a customary glance over Melbourne's cityscape.

The office block represented stunning architecture at its best...a tall, circular glass-panelled sphere designed to offer the executive offices magnificent views across the Yarra River and beyond.

It didn't take long to prioritize the messages, and

Lianne summoned a generous smile as her secretary announced the society doyenne.

As mornings went, it was a breeze. Pamela Whitcroft pontificated and prevaricated with considerable fervour, questioning each and every legal fact Lianne offered in explanation, and there was relief when the consultation concluded.

Although with it came a sense of frustration in the knowledge that Pamela Whitcroft would be back, probably before the week's end, seeking a professional opinion on the same queries from yet another junior lawyer in the firm.

Coffee…she needed the caffeine fix, and something to ease the headache pulsing behind one eye.

Routine and another client appointment took Lianne through to her customary lunch-break, which comprised a chicken salad sandwich and cold bottled water eaten at her desk in a bid to make up for lost time.

The headache still lingered. She checked her watch, then opted for some fresh air in the leafy park immediately adjacent to the office building.

Bliss, she accorded minutes later as a welcome breeze eased the tension behind her eyes, and she breathed deep, enjoying the smell of freshly cut grass mingling with the scent of garden blooms blossoming in the crisp late spring air.

Melbourne was an attractive city, with wide streets traversed by green tramcars and lined in part with broad-spreading trees. Old buildings stood next to modern architecture, providing an eclectic mix, and council planners had allocated generous space for numerous parks.

Well known for its unpredictable weather, regardless of seasonal climate, the day was mild, the skies azure with drifts of cloud and, whilst the sun provided minimum warmth, it was in direct contrast to the storm clouds and rain of the previous day.

Lianne took the path towards the central gazebo, aware of fellow office workers, students and tourists enjoying the grounds.

Couples lingered, with arms entwined and eyes only for each other.

Sudden pain twisted her stomach and she sought to ignore it…without much success as Tyler's powerful image came vividly to mind.

His tall, broad-shouldered frame, dark hair, with the sculptured facial features of a warrior.

It was three months since she had walked out of the loft apartment she'd shared with her husband of little more than a year, in a move that had seen her take a flight from his native New York to Melbourne, Australia…and home.

Three months, three weeks and two days…but who was counting? A qualified lawyer, she had a good job, had leased a nice apartment, and life was good.

Wasn't it?

In her late twenties, she was where she wanted to be, among friends, familiar territory, and far distant from her husband's high-flying lifestyle. His family, social commitments, and his supposed former lover. *Supposed*, given his denial any intimacy had occurred.

Lianne assured herself she should be pleased she'd made the decision to file for divorce. Relieved that she'd chosen to close the final page on a disastrous chapter in her life.

So why did she feel empty? And the slightly sick feeling in her stomach…what was that?

She reached the gazebo, turned, and began retracing her steps.

Eighteen months ago Tyler Benedict had entered her life, swept her off her feet, proposed, and put a ring on her finger. All in the space of a month.

He'd been her moon, the stars, an entire galaxy, and she'd loved him with every cell in her body, her heart, her soul.

So when had it all gone wrong?

It hadn't been any *one* thing, Lianne reflected as she re-entered the building foyer and took the lift to her designated floor.

More a combination of several concerns, each minor in their own way. Except they had added up, multiplied, and become something she could no longer ignore.

That had been when the arguments and accusations began, for which no apology compensated for the hurt, the pain. Looming over which there had been Mette, the tall, blonde Danish model who vowed a pre-existing *friendship* gave her licence to demand Tyler's attention. Not to mention Tyler's family, who didn't pretend to understand why he'd discarded Mette, the daughter of a lifelong family friend, for someone he'd only known a month.

The receptionist ignored the persistent burr of an incoming call. 'Michael Sloane wants to see you a.s.a.p.'

Lianne's nerves tightened a little. 'Senior, or junior?'

Michael *senior* was one of three head partners, and a pedantic, fault-finding man who could offer praise one day and verbally vilify the next.

His mercurial moods were well-known, and one staff member had been sufficiently brave to suggest it was a deliberately adopted persona as a method to keep everyone on their toes.

Whereas his son, Michael *junior*, had entered law at his father's insistence. Born with a silver spoon in his mouth, he was the spoiled only child of over-indulgent parents…a wealthy playboy who charmed clients and who had developed the fine art of appearing busy whilst burdening junior staff with his work.

'Senior.'

Lianne lifted an enquiring eyebrow and received an expressive eye-roll in response.

'Like that, huh?'

'Oh, yeah.'

Just what she needed.

Lianne took a deep breath and walked towards the separate lift accessing the penthouse.

For it was at this exalted level that the lauded echelon of senior partners occupied individual office suites, each of which comprised the office and a client lounge, manned by the partner's personal assistant and secretary.

Three men whose clientele numbered among the cream of Melbourne's wealthy society.

A requested meeting with Michael Sloane senior

succeeded in sending her vivid imagination into over-drive.

Had she made some ghastly mistake? Was she in for a metaphorical tap on the wrist for being late this morning? Or perhaps Pamela Whitcroft had filed an unflattering report following their consultation?

Focus, she admonished silently as she entered the exclusive sanctum where expensive furnishings and valuable antique furniture were the norm and original art graced wall-space.

There was a smell of lemon beeswax and fresh flowers in a tall wide vase provided a magnificent display.

'My dear, please come through.'

If Michael Sloane's personal appearance in the reception lounge came as a surprise, the *my dear* almost rendered her speechless.

She couldn't begin to think, let alone rationalise the purpose as she entered his sumptuous office.

'Make yourself comfortable.' He indicated a clutch of leather-buttoned armchairs positioned in a gracious curve, waited until she was seated, then he crossed to his executive desk and turned to face her.

Purported to be in his early sixties, his height and military bearing held formidable authority.

'I imagine you're curious as to why I've summoned you here?'

That had to be the understatement of the year!

'Surprised, Mr Sloane,' Lianne amended with polite deference.

'Oh, please…let's dispense with formality.' His smile held warmth. 'As we'll be working quite closely together, I grant you permission to use my Christian name.'

Excuse me?

'I see the need for an explanation,' he said kindly.

And then some! She felt as if she'd suddenly lost direction. Oh, heavens…*Michael*? No one got to call any of the three most senior partners by their Christian name.

'Thank you,' she managed with a calmness she was far from feeling.

'The firm has recently acquired a new client. A very influential client,' Michael Sloane elaborated. 'With international status. He already has private residential investments in Australia. He now intends to expand his property portfolio and extend his business interests here.'

It had to encompass a large scale, Lianne surmised, otherwise Michael Sloane wouldn't give it his personal attention.

'Primarily in Melbourne?'

'The client will use Melbourne as his base. He has indicated interest in Sydney, the Gold Coast, Brisbane and Cairns.'

Extensive, she allowed silently. 'His nationality?'

'American.'

Her nervous system jolted into active life, and she silently cursed herself for a fool for even thinking *Tyler*.

Tyler Benedict and that part of her life was over. She'd dealt with it, and had moved on.

Liar. Hardly a day went by when she didn't think

about her soon-to-be ex-husband...or a night when he didn't invade her dreams.

It was maddening, and frustrating as hell. A few months on it should have become...*less*. Yet his image was as vivid as the first time she had met him. Worse, she conceded, for then she'd only been consumed with the promise of what they might share...now she had the memory of endless nights spent in his arms, his touch, his kiss, and the way he could drive her beyond ecstasy.

Stop it.

There was no purpose to this. Tyler was on the other side of the world, wheeling and dealing, with Mette or some other sophisticated beauty hanging on to his every word.

He probably didn't pause to give his in-the-process-of-becoming ex-wife a thought, and if he did it would only be to shake his head at the folly of rushing into a marriage that had been doomed from the start.

'I'm flattered you've selected me to assist you,' Lianne offered quietly, and met Michael Sloane's thoughtful gaze.

'You're naturally curious as to the reason why.'

When he could have chosen his son, or any one of several eminently suitable qualified staff who'd been in the firm's employ much longer than she? 'Yes.'

Her honest response brought forth a faint smile.

'Your personnel file revealed you lived and worked for a time in the States.'

'New York.' She should feel incredibly pleased to have been plucked from relative obscurity into prominence as Michael Sloane's assistant. So why was she getting a strange feeling about all of this? It didn't make sense.

'You will, of course, receive an increased salary package.' He mentioned a figure that was more than generous. 'Together with certain privileges.'

A new office, her own secretary…it was all a bit much. And *Michael*…who else but Shane Everton and Dante Shell called Michael Sloane *Michael*?

'Thank you.'

'You will report to this level, as from tomorrow. A copy of the client's file will be made available, and you will take instructions from me.'

'I understand. It would help if I could ascertain some background information on the client.' It would also help her to breathe more easily to eliminate Tyler from the equation.

He checked his watch. 'You'll get to meet him. I expect my personal assistant to announce his arrival within minutes.'

The communication module on his desk gave a discreet burr and he reached for the receiver. 'Yes, show him through.'

Lianne rose to her feet and turned to face the door, aware of an elevated sense of nerves.

There was a split second when Caroline James stood in the aperture, then she stepped to one side, her smile professionally faultless.

'Tyler Benedict.'

For a mindless few seconds everything came to a screeching halt…including Lianne's heartbeat.

It was almost as if she was viewing a Technicolor movie and someone hit the *pause* button.

Dear God.

It was only a week since she'd indicated her intention to set divorce proceedings in motion. Seven days during which she'd agonised over his possible reaction.

Was he intent on playing a deliberate game? Or was his presence here *now* merely coincidence?

Even *thinking* it might be the former set her nerves into a jangling mess.

'Tyler. I trust you had a good flight?'

'Thank you. Yes.'

The sound of his voice, pure New York drawl, curled round her nerve-endings and tugged a little.

Lianne forced herself to meet his gaze, aware of just how much effort it took to retain it.

He looked…incredible, she conceded.

In his late thirties, the European tailoring fit his tall broad frame as if it had been made especially for him. Which it probably had. He possessed an innate grace that reminded her of a sleek jungle animal, all muscular power and a waiting, watchful quality that boded ill for an unwary prey.

Broad-boned facial structure, piercing grey eyes and a mouth that promised a thousand sensual delights.

And had delivered, Lianne reflected, remembering all too easily how it had felt to move beneath him, over him. To become one, and forget who or what she was…except *his*. Only his.

The warmth of his smile, the way his eyes had softened whenever he looked at her…the antithesis of the impersonal demeanour now evident, for there was a hardness apparent, a ruthlessness that was almost chilling.

'My assistant, Lianne Marshall.' Michael Sloane effected the introduction, and for a millisecond she thought she glimpsed a primitive darkening in Tyler's grey eyes. Then it was gone and she was left to wonder if it had merely been a trick of the light.

Tyler inclined his head fractionally, his expression impossible to read as he subjected her to a lingering, almost searching, appraisal, taking in her petite frame with its slender curves, attractive facial features, upswept ash-blonde hair, the sapphire-blue eyes.

'Lianne,' he acknowledged with drawled politeness.

'Please—' Michael senior indicated a selection of leather chairs '—take a seat.'

Awareness fizzed through her veins, activating every nerve-end until her whole body *hummed* with sensual heat. A reaction that brought a sense of helpless anger…with herself, *him*.

Act. And remember to breathe. Slowly.

You can do this, she assured herself silently.

Tyler chose the chair next to her own, and this close she could sense the subtle tones of his cologne mingling with the faint clean smell of freshly laundered clothes.

There was something else, an indefinable essence that was intensely male and uniquely his.

It attacked the fragile tenure of her control and tested it. She didn't like it, didn't want it…just as she would rather be anywhere but *here*.

Except she was sufficiently mature to separate her business and private lives. *Wasn't she?*

And this was solely business. Following this initial meeting, it was doubtful she'd have much contact with Tyler.

Tyler would consult with Michael Sloane. Her participation would be restricted to behind the scenes, checking documentation, title searches, liaising, making endless phone calls and relaying all relevant information to her boss.

How difficult could it be?

Who do you think you're kidding?

Tyler's manner was pleasant, but only a fool would fail to detect the underlying steel as he outlined his *modus operandi*, his expectations of Sloane, Everton, Shell and Associates, and Michael Sloane senior in particular.

Tyler was *there*, in her face, and his presence taxed her composure to the limit.

It came as a tremendous relief when he brought the consultation to a close.

Every minute seemed to have crawled by at snail's pace, and she hid her surprise as a surreptitious glance at her watch revealed only twenty minutes had passed.

'Michael.' Tyler inclined as he rose to his feet, then he turned towards her. 'Lianne.'

She forced herself to meet his gaze, glimpsed the coolness in those dark grey eyes, and matched it for a few seconds before she inclined her head.

It was over…for now. Impossible not to add that qualification as Michael senior crossed the room, opened the door and ushered Tyler into the care of his personal assistant.

Lianne's relief was palpable, although she managed

to disguise it as her boss closed the door and took a seat behind his impressive desk.

'The client has orchestrated a punishing schedule.'

Lianne could almost visualize Michael senior using a mental calculator as he added up an obscene amount in legal fees.

Instinct warned that Tyler's presence in Australia, *Melbourne*, and specifically his choice of Sloane, Everton, Shell and Associates as his legal advisors wasn't coincidental.

Which meant he'd kept tabs on her.

Wondering *why* occupied her mind for what remained of the afternoon, while she fought peak hour traffic to suburban Brighton, and as she rode the lift to her apartment.

The marriage was over, divorce was her considered option, they hadn't exactly parted as friends, and she'd refused to take any one of his phone calls.

What hellish game was Tyler intent on playing?

CHAPTER TWO

LIANNE inserted the key into the lock and breathed a sigh of contentment as she entered the apartment and closed the door behind her.

With automatic movements she slid off her stilettos and unbuttoned her jacket with one hand whilst discarding her briefcase with the other.

A cool drink, a shower, comfortable clothes, then she'd assemble a salad, add some protein, and relax.

It had, she determined as she padded into the kitchen, been a fraught day.

The contents of her refrigerator offered a few choices, and she snagged a bottle of mineral water, twisted the top free, then drank long before capping it as she wandered into the lounge.

She adored this apartment…furnished, modern, situated on a high floor with a fabulous view and comprising a spacious lounge, dining room, kitchen, three bedrooms, utilities.

The rent was affordable, and with the addition of a desk and bookshelves she'd converted the smaller bedroom into a study, leaving the main bedroom and a guest room.

She'd added a few personal touches, flower pots on the balcony and a small wrought-iron table and chair where she often had breakfast. Indoors there were vases holding displays of silk flowers and prints adorned the walls.

Hers, by virtue of a generous lease renewable subject to agent approval.

A faint sound broke the silence. For a moment she thought it came from inside the apartment, except that was crazy. No one would break in…surely? Security measures made it difficult, and besides—

There it was again. This time it sounded like the sliding of a shower door…and it came from the direction of the main bathroom.

Lianne felt every muscle tense.

There was someone inside the apartment.

She knew the drill…phone the triple digit emergency number.

With considerable care she retraced her steps into the lounge, opened her briefcase, retrieved her cellphone, then keyed in the numbers.

'Police,' she directed quietly, and was about to state her name and address when the cellphone was taken from her hand.

'That won't be necessary.'

The voice was male, its New York drawl achingly familiar, and her anger rose to fever pitch in the few seconds it took to face Tyler.

'What are you doing *here*?' She lashed out a fist and connected with his shoulder. 'Dammit! How did you get in?'

He was close, much too close, damp, and the towel carelessly secured at his hips exposed a superbly muscled chest beneath broad shoulders, enviable biceps, powerful thighs…and far too much naked flesh.

'With a key.'

She wanted to move back a pace, but angry pride forbade it. 'Which you secured…how, and from whom?'

Building security was…*secure*. It had been one of the major factors which attracted her to this particular group of apartments.

'By right of ownership,' Tyler informed, watching the twin flags of colour along each cheekbone as realisation dawned. He read and interpreted each fleeting emotion, saw the anger deepen as she did the maths.

'The apartment.' Which made him her landlord.

'The building,' he corrected mildly.

Now why did that surprise her?

It explained the low rental she'd thought too good to be true in this particular locale. It also brought a host of queries tumbling from her lips.

'A set-up from the start? What did you do?' Her eyes flashed blue fire. 'Circulate my photo to every realtor in the entire city?' He was capable of more, much more. Her voice held bitter resignation. 'Chance didn't enter the equation, did it?'

'No.'

Lianne banked down the anger. 'Tell me,' she continued with seeming coolness. 'Did you employ a private detective or a bodyguard?'

'I ensured your protection.'

His voice held a certain bleakness and without thought her hand flew in an upward arc and connected with his cheek in a resounding slap. 'How *dare* you?'

A muscle bunched at the edge of his jaw and his eyes were dark and dangerous. 'Are you done?'

He could have caught hold of her hand mid-flight. The fact he hadn't surprised her.

'Not even close.' She drew in a deep breath, then released it slowly. 'My position with Sloane, Everton, Shell and Associates?'

His gaze was direct and unwavering. 'You gained on your own merit.'

It was impossible to dampen down an edge of sarcasm. 'Small mercy.' It sickened her to think he'd received reports detailing her life since she left him. Where she worked, lived, who she met and what she did.

'I take care of what is mine,' Tyler assured with dangerous silkiness.

Nerves tightened into a painful ball inside her stomach. His words created an image of long nights and the scent, texture and feel of his body beneath her hands, her mouth. The way he could drive her wild...dear heaven, beyond *wild* with a lovemaking that broke all barriers. Fast and passionately *driven*, or long, tender and slow...he had the power to take her places she hadn't known existed. Sensual nirvana, in all its connotations.

She'd thought it was enough. More than enough. Nothing, she'd imagined, could touch them.

Except reality intervened, intruding with a dogged persistence impossible to ignore. *Mette*...a tall blue-eyed blonde Danish model, known only by her Christian name, who'd built an international reputation gracing the European catwalks, and Tyler's former lover...or so Mette had said. A woman who consciously chose to remain at the forefront, highly visible at almost every social function Tyler and Lianne had attended.

Now Lianne's chin lifted and her eyes seared his. 'I'm no longer *yours*.'

He was silent for what seemed an age, and his voice when he spoke was dangerously soft. 'No?'

Could he read minds? See beneath her façade and determine the jangle of nerves creating havoc with her equilibrium? Know *he* was the cause? All because of the exigent sensual chemistry they had shared?

Except it was more than that…much more.

'You can't stay here,' Lianne refuted adamantly. To have him share the apartment, even for the briefest time, wasn't an option.

He lifted a hand and threaded fingers through his hair. 'There are three bedrooms; surely you don't begrudge me the use of one of them?'

'You have to be kidding.'

He looked…tired. The result of a long flight, little sleep, and back-to-back business appointments?

'A base, somewhere I can spend a night in between flights.'

'There are places which cater for overnight guests,' she voiced evenly. 'They're called hotels. Book a suite.'

'Why do that, when I own an apartment?' he queried with deceptive mildness.

'I have a legally binding lease.' She met his gaze with fearless disregard. 'Nowhere in the fine print does it say I have to allow the landlord free residence at any time.'

'Might I remind you we're still husband and wife?'

'Bound by a marriage certificate that hasn't counted for anything in months?'

'Your choice,' Tyler asserted silkily. 'Not mine.'

'How can you say that?' Lianne demanded in disbelief.

'Easily. You were the one to walk.'

'*You* cheated,' she flung wretchedly, and saw his expression harden.

'My answer is the same now as it was then.'

The memory of their argument was hauntingly vivid. Too vivid. 'Get dressed, and get out.'

One eyebrow rose. 'I pose no threat.'

That's what you think. Even the mere thought of him sleeping in a room close to her own was enough to send her pulse-rate rocketing.

Given the circumstances of their separation, a few months down the track should have eased the heartache and diminished the need. It hadn't, and she hated him for it, hated herself.

'Or is it yourself you're afraid of?'

He was right on the button, she conceded, and held down the anger. 'That doesn't deserve an answer.'

'A bed, Lianne.'

'As long as you understand it won't be mine.'

One eyebrow rose. 'I wasn't aware I implied it might be.'

He was cool, way too cool, and she didn't like it. He possessed a well-deserved reputation in the business arena for being a ruthless adversary. Someone to have as a friend, never an enemy.

To her, he was neither. Yet she felt she was treading

on eggshells, wary, and *hating* the heat she tried so hard to subdue.

She was over him. Totally. Wasn't that why she intended to seek a divorce? To be rid of him, so she could move on with her life?

So why in hell was her pulse racing to a quickened beat? Or her mind in conflict with the dictates of her body?

It was an itch, an urge, motivated by the memory of what had been. A time when they couldn't keep their hands off each other, as if what they shared would never be enough…for either of them.

The fast passion, the long slow loving…

Stop it. The words remained locked in her throat, a silent scream that didn't, couldn't, find voice.

'You're doing this deliberately, aren't you?' Lianne demanded at last, and saw his eyebrow arch a little higher.

'What, precisely?'

'Taking control, creating a diabolical situation.' Her chin tilted a little. 'Tell me, are you doing it just for the hell of it?'

'Why make something simple into such a big deal?'

'Because *simple* doesn't form part of your vocabulary!'

Temper ran warm colour over her cheekbones and lit her eyes with a fiery gleam. He wanted to reach out and trail his fingers over the heat, to feel it, then cup her face and cover her mouth with his own.

This close he was intensely aware of her, the clean smell of her hair, the soft floral perfume emanating from her skin…a subtle evocative scent that was essentially *her*. It was something she hadn't sought to change, and it pleased him.

'You think not?'

His drawled query made her edgy. So too did his body language. She wanted to take a backwards step, put some distance between them…except she stubbornly remained where she was.

'Why are you here?'

His gaze didn't shift from hers. 'In Melbourne?'

He was toying with her, stringing out the play. It was an acquired skill. 'That, too.'

'I made my purpose apparent in Michael Sloane's office.'

'So you did,' she managed with wry cynicism. 'You intend to buy up property, residential and industrial, gut existing buildings or tear them down and rebuild. You're good at it.' His success was the stuff of legends. She took a deep breath, then demanded, 'Why *here*?'

Tyler's gaze lanced hers. 'You have an objection?'

'Several.'

'Perhaps you'd care to name them?' His voice was pure silk.

She wanted to hit him, and curled each hand into a fist in a bid for restraint. 'Abandon the game, why don't you, and cut to the chase.'

He waited a beat. 'I made the decision to establish an Australian base.'

Her head tilted a little as she regarded him. 'You expect me to believe that, when every move you make is a calculated manoeuvre?'

'What would you have me say, Lianne?'

'The truth might be a start.'

His silence seemed to stretch too long, and it took courage to hold his unwavering gaze.

'I have never lied to you.'

'Been there, done that,' she reminded, and saw his jaw tighten.

'And you didn't believe me then, any more than you do now,' he stated with a degree of cynicism, and saw her chin tilt in defiance.

'The evidence was stacked against you.'

'By a woman whose word you chose to trust over mine,' Tyler reminded with hateful ease.

'That's supposed to change what happened? Forgive and forget?' She was on a roll. '*Please*. Give me a break.'

Her eyes raked his powerful frame in deliberate appraisal. 'I'm going to take a shower. I want you dressed and out of here by the time I'm done.'

It was a great exit line. One of the best. She only hoped he didn't guess her nerves were a chaotic mess as she walked away from him.

Seconds later she carefully closed the bedroom door, then began to undress. Her fingers shook as she unfastened her skirt and she drew a deep steadying breath as she peeled off her tights, discarded underwear, then crossed to the *en suite* bathroom.

A leisurely shower would do wonders in easing the tenseness from her body, and she'd shampoo her hair. By the time she emerged, Tyler should be gone.

Half an hour later, towelled dry, she used the hair-drier, snagged jeans and a singlet top, then she twisted the length of her hair into a careless knot atop her head and emerged into the hallway.

The door to the guest bedroom was closed, and she swung it open automatically, choking back a sound that was a mixture of shock, irritation and anger at the sight of Tyler sprawled face down on top of the bed, asleep, with only a towel hitched at his waist.

The powerful musculature captured her gaze and held it with magnetic force as she lingered on the breadth of his shoulders, the flex of sinew, the strong spine beneath the golden tanned skin.

There was the temptation to move close and trace each ridge of muscle and vertebra indentation, to caress the smooth skin and thread her fingers through his dark tousled hair. To touch her lips to his nape...

Dear heaven, where had that come from?

Get a grip. Such wayward thoughts led to madness. She had to get him out of here. Now.

'Tyler.'

Calling his name brought no response whatsoever, and she bit back an unladylike oath as she crossed the room and shook the bed, then *him*.

To no avail, for he didn't move.

'Damn you, Tyler.' The muttered condemnation held a mix of angry frustration as she grabbed hold of his shoulders and put strength into shaking him *hard*.

'*Wake up.*'

A hand snaked out and closed over her forearm. 'Tell me there's a fire or some other life-threatening disaster,' he muttered in a gravelly voice. 'Otherwise get out and let me sleep.'

Lianne tried to tug her arm free without success, for

he merely tightened his grip. 'Get up, get dressed, and get the hell out of my apartment.'

Tyler effected a slow body roll to lie facing her, his eyes impossibly dark as he met her angry gaze.

'We've already done that.'

She wrenched her arm and growled a husky expletive when he failed to release it.

His lips formed a mocking smile. 'My mother would argue with you.' He sounded indolently amused and it irked her unbearably.

'Let me go, dammit!' The temptation to lash out at him was irresistible, and she gave a startled gasp as he tugged her forward.

One second she was standing, the next she was fighting to retain her balance. Something he allowed her to do...just. Yet the threat of intent was there, the ease with which he held control apparent as he held her there, poised between tipping her down on to the bed or letting her go.

Time was held suspended as everything faded into the background. There was only the man, the moment, and a vivid reminder of the exigent chemistry they had shared.

Lianne was almost afraid to breathe as sensual awareness pierced her feminine core and began radiating through her body, searing every nerve, heating her flesh until she felt as if she was on fire.

For months she'd led a celibate existence, alternately hating *him* and learning to live without him.

Until today she'd thought she was on the path towards self-survival. Yet all it had taken was one look and she was pitched back to the pleasure and the pain of having loved him with her heart and soul.

She couldn't, *wouldn't* go there again.

Lianne banked down confusion and resorted to anger as she made another attempt to wrench out of his grasp. 'What in hell do you think you're doing?'

Did she realise how beautiful she was? Hair like spun silk, fine cream-textured skin and eyes the colour of brilliant sapphire. Know how easily she could arouse him? Just looking at her did it for him every time.

'Defending myself,' he drawled with a tinge of humour. He'd missed their verbal sparring, her spontaneity, warmth, her fire. Dammit, *everything* that was *her*.

'So you should,' she said fiercely. 'Right now I could kill you.'

'Have mercy.' His voice held a gravelly quality. 'I haven't slept in thirty-six hours.'

He watched the fleeting emotions chase across her expressive features as he released her arm.

It was still there, the sensual chemistry they shared, simmering beneath the surface. For each of them. Knowing it was enough.

Tyler rolled on to his stomach, crossed his arms on the pillow, then lowered his head. 'Close the door on your way out.'

Lianne remained where she was for a few seconds, speechless. Then the anger returned and with it the urge to do him bodily harm.

'Don't,' he warned with dangerous silkiness. 'Unless you want to deal with the consequences.'

His meaning was unmistakable, and the air between them became electric. So much so, she consciously held her breath as her senses turned traitor and consumed her body with need.

It was all too easy to recall how it had felt to be caught up in the sensual thrall they'd once shared. Possessed by each other to such a degree where nothing else had existed...only them, consumed by a sexual magic uniquely their own.

There was a part of her that wanted, *craved*, to turn back the clock, sink down and take him on a wild ride that would leave them both shaken and spent.

Are you insane? The silent voice of reason kicked in and broke the highly volatile thread of conflicting thought.

It was a madness she couldn't afford, nor could she allow herself the luxury of remembering what they used to share.

Tyler had severed that special bond. It was over, long gone...dead. *Wasn't it?*

She had to admit that her body was in conflict with the dictates of her brain. And she didn't like it.

The temptation to heap ire on his hapless head was paramount. To throw caution to the wind and let her anger have full rein.

Except that would play right into his hands, and she refused to go there.

Instead she derived a certain satisfaction in retreating without a further word.

It indicated he hadn't got to her, and it was *she*, not he, who was in control.

A fallacy, despite the façade. For inside she was a

trembling mass of shattered nerves, swept back to a place she'd sworn never to visit again.

For the past few months she'd enjoyed the relative calm her life had become. The routine of work, the company of a few good friends. She didn't need a man in her life.

Especially not a soon-to-be ex-husband!

With care she turned and quietly left the room, closing the door behind her with an almost silent click. Then she walked calmly out to the kitchen, fixed a salad and took the plate out on to the balcony to sit staring out over the panoramic vista as the sun sank slowly towards the horizon.

Food didn't interest her, and after desultorily forking a few mouthfuls she discarded her plate and contemplated what her next step would be.

Attempting to physically remove Tyler wasn't an option. And phoning the police and citing a domestic incident was overkill.

Whether she liked it or not, Tyler was there for the night.

So what? a devilish imp prompted. *Deal with it.*

She could phone one of a few close friends and suggest they meet for coffee, take in a movie. Or she could put in a few hours on her laptop.

Work, she decided as she tidied the kitchen, then she filched a diet cola from the refrigerator and took it into the room she used as a home office.

It was almost midnight when she saved the file and closed the laptop. Her shoulders ached and she felt weary beyond belief.

A hot shower should have acted as a precursor to easily acquired sleep. Instead she lay between cool sheets, staring at the shadowed ceiling until exhaustion brought a few hours of blissful oblivion.

CHAPTER THREE

LIANNE woke feeling as if she'd spent the night fighting a disturbing dream. Worse, her mirrored reflection merely endorsed it.

A shower did nothing to lift her mood, and even the skilful application of make-up couldn't disguise the dark hollows beneath her eyes.

There were several stylish business suits in her wardrobe, and she riffled through the selection, chose red, signifying power...let's face it, she needed all the help she could get! The straight skirt enhanced her slim curves and the fitted jacket could be worn without a blouse.

With her hair swept into a loose chignon, stiletto-heeled pumps, minimum jewellery, she was done.

Coffee, black, sweet and strong, had to provide a kick-start to the day, and she drew in a deep breath, then released it as she opened her bedroom door.

Please God, Tyler had already left, she offered in silent prayer as she made her way to the kitchen.

Except the Deity wasn't listening.

Tyler was seated at the breakfast bar, cutlery in hand as he did justice to a plate of grilled bacon, eggs, toast, and freshly made coffee.

Dressed in dark tailored trousers, a deep blue shirt unbuttoned at the neck, he looked every inch the powerful magnate. His jacket lay carelessly tossed over a nearby chair, topped by a tie.

He glanced up as she appeared and she suffered his leisurely appraisal.

'I was about to come wake you.' His drawl held a tinge of humour as he remembered just how he'd stirred her into wakefulness...and her generous response.

'These days I have an electronic alarm clock.' Smooth, very smooth. And before her first dose of caffeine, too.

The edge of his mouth curved. 'There's extra bacon and eggs.'

Lianne met his gaze with equanimity. 'Thanks, but no thanks.'

He replaced his cutlery and pushed his plate to one side. 'Because you've switched to fruit and yoghurt?'

Because I'm not taking anything from you. 'Charm isn't going to work.'

Tyler picked up his cup, drained the contents and stood up. 'I need to get to the airport.'

She watched idly as he fixed the top button of his shirt, added his tie, then caught up his jacket and shrugged it on with a lithe grace she'd always admired in him.

He had the co-ordinated movements of a man at the peak of physical fitness, fluid, with enviable muscle flex and total balance. Controlled strength, she added, aware of its gentleness...as well as its power. Knowing she'd experienced both.

There had been a time when he'd have closed the distance and pulled her in, lowered his head and taken possession of her mouth in memory of the night they'd shared…and anticipation of the night ahead.

Now he simply collected his briefcase from the foot of the table and offered her a piercing glance. 'Have a good day.'

She had a need for retaliation. 'I'd rather not see you again.'

One eyebrow slanted. 'Difficult, while Michael Sloane handles my file.'

'Something you deliberately set up in order to bug me?'

The edge of his mouth twitched a little. 'Is it working?'

'Not a snowflake's chance in Hades,' she managed with succinct cynicism.

His soft laughter almost unleashed the anger simmering beneath the surface of her control, and she held on to it…just, watching as he turned and walked from the apartment.

Lianne felt the need to throw something…anything, just to have the satisfaction of hearing it shatter. Except then she'd have to clean up the mess, she'd be down a plate, cup…and besides, she didn't have the time.

Instead she filled a cup with coffee, added sugar, and sipped it contemplatively as she tried to ignore the plate of bacon and eggs warming in the oven.

Hunger won out. Although she only ate one piece of bacon and forked two mouthfuls of egg before reluctantly dispensing the rest down the food disposal unit. It was the principle of the thing, she assured herself silently. And being unwilling to allow Tyler to win at anything over which she had some control.

Minutes later she consigned china and cutlery into the dishwasher, then she collected her briefcase and took the lift down to the underground car park and slid into her Mini Cooper.

Traffic was heavy, providing delays at various intersections *en route* into the city. It gave Lianne time to lapse into reflective thought. Until a horn blast alerted her to a change in the lights, a moving line of cars, thus galvanising her into action…only to have the car engine stall and suffer annoyed embarrassment at holding up traffic until it kicked into life again.

Dammit, she silently berated herself. *Focus!*

Something she forced herself to do throughout the day. Although it was difficult to dispense Tyler from her mind when most of her work centred around his business interests.

Word of Lianne's promotion had swiftly circulated and with such a large compilation of staff undercurrents were inevitable, together with conflicting personality traits well-hidden beneath the surface of polite civility.

While Lianne knew she was good at her job, she was all too aware there was speculation as to why *her* over and above anyone else?

What would happen if she set the cat among the pigeons and owned up to being the wife of Sloane, Everton, Shell and Associates' new influential client? Worse, that it had been Tyler Benedict who'd used his manipulative skills to this effect?

Although *wife* was a mere legal technicality soon to be remedied.

Lianne was in the midst of keying data into a laptop when there was a tap at her open door, and she glanced up to see Michael Sloane junior walk into her office.

'Genuinely busy, or merely making it look as if you are?'

The boss's son, who could, if he tried, be quite a pleasant young man. Except he had delusions of grandeur about his own worth, his position as a senior partner's son, delighted in innuendo and his ability to charm the opposite sex.

The fact he'd been trying to charm her from day one merely whetted his determination to succeed. Except she wasn't willing to play…with him, or any man.

'A workload I need to finish before the day's close,' Lianne offered matter-of-factly. 'Is there something I can help you with?'

He moved into the room and slid into a chair opposite her desk. 'Yes.'

'Spit it out. I don't have time to play twenty questions.'

'I love it when you talk tough.'

Please, she offered silently. I don't need this.

A quiet steadying breath did little to soothe her impatience. 'Be specific, Michael.'

'As specific as you like. For starters, you can—'

'Want me to spell out the definition of harassment in the workplace?'

'You malign me.' He looked suitably hurt. 'I was going to ask you to join me for dinner tonight.'

She took a moment to observe him, the playboy good looks, the manner that came from being the only child of wealthy, highly eminent professional parents who'd obviously over-indulged him from birth. Something he'd used and abused through his scholastic years into adulthood if his level of self-assurance was any indication. Women fawned over him because of who he was, his connections, and what he could do for them.

'Michael.' Her voice sounded vaguely weary, even to her own ears. Too much stress and not enough sleep, she reasoned as she aimed for politeness. 'When are you going to get it that I'm not interested?'

His smile held smug certainty. 'Persistence, Lianne. It's my forte.'

Patience. She needed it, like right now. 'I'm a lost cause,' she managed evenly. 'Go find someone else to play with.'

'Why, when you present such a challenge?'

'You're wasting your time.'

'Maybe I should be the judge of that.'

'Go take a hike…please,' she added.

He inclined his head in a gesture of mockery and rose to his feet. 'I give in…for now. Tune in, same time, same place, for the next scintillating episode in this ongoing drama.'

She almost laughed.

'Gotcha.'

His soft taunt had Lianne pointing a hand in the direction of the door. 'Go.'

He went. And only dedicated application ensured she completed the day's quota of work on time.

It was good to close down her laptop, collect her briefcase and head for the lift.

A workout in the apartment building's gymnasium, followed by a swim in the adjoining pool, would ease the kinks in her shoulders, her neck. After which she'd fix herself an omelette, research a law study project, and aim for an early night.

Tyler's overnight stay had been a one-off. Consequently there was no reason for the faint edge of nervous tension that increased with every kilometre traversed *en route* to suburban Brighton.

Get a grip, she chastised silently as she swept her car down beneath her apartment building and slid into her designated parking bay.

The thought that Tyler could have returned to her apartment caused her to jab the lift call-button with unnecessary force, and she silently plotted dire consequences, only to discard them as blissful quietness greeted her, followed by relief.

The tension eased and Lianne worked at dispensing it altogether as she completed a punishing gym workout. Then she took advantage of the heated indoor pool before drying off and pulling on sweats.

A shower, she mused as she re-entered her apartment, and took her time over it, luxuriating in the warm pulsing water, the delicately scented shampoo and soap.

Comfort determined her choice of apparel, and she stepped into thong briefs, added shorts, dispensed with a bra and pulled on a skinny-knit top, then she twisted her damp hair into a loose knot.

Food, she decided as she exited her bedroom...and bumped into a solid male frame.

'What in hell...?'

Strong hands closed over her shoulders, steadying her as she automatically began to struggle.

'It's OK. Relax.'

The New York drawl was all too familiar, so too was the sight, sense and smell of him. The slight woodsy tone of his cologne, fresh clothing and...dear God, the way her senses flew on to full alert at his presence.

'What are you doing here?'

'We've already been there, done that.' Tyler's voice held wry amusement and he saw, *felt* the anger rise up and consume her.

'So?' Lianne demanded as she tried to step back from him and failed miserably. 'We'll do it again. You're not supposed to be here!'

He'd discarded his suit jacket and his arms felt warm and muscularly hard beneath her hands. In a flash she discarded her grip as if burnt by flame.

'I don't recall stating I wouldn't be back,' he declared with indolent ease.

No, she reflected hollowly. He hadn't. 'I assumed—'

'I'd observe your request and retreat?'

Oh, hell. *'Yes.'*

His smile didn't reach his eyes. 'Not in this lifetime.'

'Why?' Angry frustration clouded her features. 'Why can't you move on and leave me alone?' she demanded.

'As you have?'

Had she? Dammit, she'd moved a continent away from him in order to survive...emotionally, mentally. But she wasn't *alive*. Not in the way she'd been when she was with him.

Then, he'd been her true love. Her soul mate. The other half of her whole. She'd lived for his smile, his touch, the magic that had been theirs alone.

He *knew* her...how she thought, what she felt, everything about her. And all it took was a look. Extra sensory perception at its zenith. Or two souls so in tune with each other there was no need for words.

Now, they each wore a protective shield, and what had been was well hidden.

'I walked out of your life,' Lianne managed quietly. 'Is it too much to ask you to stay out of mine?'

'Yes.'

'*Why?*' She closed her eyes, then opened them again to see his head descend.

Her lips parted in protest, except no words emerged as his head descended and he took possession of her mouth in a kiss that wreaked havoc with her defences.

It was heat and light, all sensual warmth and passion as it shattered the tenuous hold of her control.

She could close her eyes and imagine the last few months had never been, and the temptation to give herself up to sensation was almost more than she could bear.

Worse, because she wanted to...desperately. Just hold on, and go wherever he chose to take her.

What are you thinking? an inner voice screeched silently. To travel that path was madness. A madness she could ill afford, for it would return her to a time and place in her life she'd spent long months trying so hard to forget.

Tyler sensed the moment she tried to gain control, and it behoved his strength of will that he let her. He could, he knew, use subtle persuasion to his advantage, trail his mouth to the sensitive curve of her neck and savour the rapidly beating pulse, nip it with the edge of his teeth, and slide his hands beneath the skinny top she was wearing.

Seek the firm roundness of her breasts and skim his fingers back and forth over their taut peaks. Take first one, then the other into his mouth and feel her tremble.

Instead, he softened the kiss, slowly withdrawing until his mouth brushed hers, gently, back and forth, before raising his head to look at her.

She appeared slightly dazed, her mouth faintly swollen, and her eyes were dark with passion.

For a moment he almost tossed caution aside, except she possessed an air of fragility that touched him deep inside.

'That's why,' Tyler said gently, releasing her.

Lianne felt her body sway for an instant before she straightened and took a backward step.

Dear Lord in heaven.

She lifted shaky fingers to her mouth, unable to tear her gaze away from his, and for a few long seconds neither moved.

'I think you'd better leave,' she managed quietly and almost flinched as he reached out and cupped her chin.

'Have you eaten?'

Food? He was talking about *food*?

'Tyler—'

He pressed a thumb over her lips. 'Order in, or go out. Your choice.'

She shook her head. 'I don't think—'

'The simple sharing of a meal.' He traced the curve of her lower lip. 'We can do that, surely?'

She drew in a breath, then let it go in an attempt to regain her composure. Minutes ago…it *was* only *minutes*, wasn't it?…she'd been ready to rage at him. What had happened to that?

'I have plans.' She could invent some.

'To wash your hair?' Tyler queried, straight-faced.

Lianne doubted any woman had used an excuse not to date him. 'Zoe. We're going to take in a movie.'

'Zoe rang while you were in the shower. Your movie date with her is tomorrow night.'

Damn. She'd been found out. 'I don't want to go anywhere with you.'

'We both need to eat. Why not together in pleasant surroundings?'

'A little wine, candlelight…and a seduction attempt?' she countered with a tinge of mockery and saw his slow smile.

'I haven't come close to seducing you…yet.'

'And you won't.'

Tyler traced an idle finger down the slope of her nose. 'Not tonight.'

'Not *any* night.'

'Go change,' he bade easily.

'If I do, will you agree to book into a hotel?'

He was unable to resist the temptation to tease. 'With you?'

Lianne felt like screaming with vexation. 'Dammit, *no.*'

He regarded her carefully. 'No.'

'I don't want you here.' She hated the slight desperation in her voice.

'Too bad.'

'I could phone the police and have them evict you.'

'Make the call.'

'Whereupon you'll explain you own the apartment, a marriage exists between us, there's been a domestic misunderstanding which is in the process of being settled?'

His eyes gleamed with wry humour. 'That's about the sum of it.'

'You make it easy for me to hate you.'

'I'll take an honest emotion over indifference.'

Indifference was the last thing she felt for him, and she hated that he knew it.

As much as she wanted to scream and rage against him, she aimed for icy cynicism. 'Really?' She raised one eyebrow and regarded him steadily. 'Dinner.' She could do dinner *and* feign indifference. Just for the hell of it and to prove to herself that she could.

'There's a restaurant in Toorak.' She named it, adding, 'If they're booked, just mention my name.' She waited a beat. 'Lianne *Marshall.*' It gave her immense satisfaction to see his eyes harden, and she added, 'Half an hour?'

He resisted the temptation to crush that soft mouth

with his own. Instead, he let her walk away. There was time, and he intended to take it slow.

Tyler lifted a hand and raked fingers through his hair as he made for the guest bedroom, where he took a shower and dressed in dark trousers, blue shirt and silk tie, then added a jacket.

Lianne was waiting for him when he emerged into the lounge, and his senses quickened as he took in her sleek upswept hair, the exquisite make-up.

Stunning, he accorded silently, admiring the black silk evening trousers and camisole, killer heels, the silver cobwebby shawl draped low over her shoulders.

Her jewellery was limited to a watch and a slender diamond drop pendant. Neither of which had been gifts from him.

She could easily afford both items. She didn't lack money, he'd seen to it that a generous personal allowance was paid into her bank account each month. There was also her salary package.

Lianne collected her keys and queried briskly, 'Do you want to drive, or shall I?'

'I'll drive, you navigate.'

CHAPTER FOUR

THEY took his car, a sleek black Porsche he'd bought the previous day. It was like the man, Lianne accorded silently. Dark, fast and dangerous.

The restaurant was well-known for its fine cuisine, excellent service and expensive wines. Situated in a small one-way street, accessed through a plate glass door, the interior held an ambience all its own.

Seated, Tyler deferred to her choice of wine, and perused the menu before selecting a starter and main course, while Lianne settled for a starter.

'Not hungry?'

'No.' She was battening down nerves, hating the emotions tangling themselves into an impossible mess.

It was crazy. Being here was crazy. What on earth had possessed her to agree to share dinner with him?

Manipulative tactics on his part, and determination on hers to prove she could play him at his own game and win.

The waiter presented the wine, poured a sample, then, gaining approval, he part-filled both goblets.

'What now, Tyler?' Lianne took a sip of wine. 'Polite conversation? *How was your day?*' Her voice held a tinge of mockery. 'Meaningless words to fill a void?'

'Why not meaningful?'

'There's the thing.' She leaned back in her chair and pretended speculative contemplation. 'So many choices.' Her eyes held his with unblinking solemnity. 'Shall I begin, or will you?'

Tyler inclined his head. 'By all means…you.'

'Ah, is this wise, do you think?'

'Wisdom isn't an issue.'

She toyed with the stem of her goblet. 'What *is* the issue, Tyler?'

'Reconciliation,' he drawled. 'Ours.'

Oh, my. Such succinct honesty captured her breath and held it hostage for several long seconds. 'That's not going to happen.'

'We share something special.'

'Did,' she corrected. 'As in past tense.'

'Wrong,' he assured with quiet emphasis.

Lianne didn't attempt to misunderstand him. 'Sexual chemistry?'

'That, too.'

'It's been months, Tyler,' she reminded with wry cynicism. 'If you thought what we shared was worth saving…what kept you?'

He regarded her steadily. 'You refused to take my calls, and if I did manage to connect you hung up on me.'

The waiter arrived and presented their starters, then he discreetly disappeared.

'And your point is?'

'I wanted to fly out here and drag you back to New York.' Except events had conspired against him.

'Kidnapping is a serious crime, bearing in mind I'd never have gone with you willingly.'

'That did occur to me.'

'How astute,' she accorded sweetly.

'My father was killed in a car accident.'

The news shocked her. 'I'm so sorry,' she managed with genuine sincerity. 'When?'

'Three days after you left.'

Lianne closed her eyes briefly, then opened them again. She could only imagine his mother's pain, *his*. Not to mention the added business responsibilities necessary to ensure that Blair Benedict's industrial empire suffered minimum setback during the transition period in directorship.

It didn't help that she hadn't known. Hadn't had the opportunity to express her condolences.

'I'm sorry,' she reiterated with genuine remorse.

'Then there was Mette.'

'The incredible feline with claws of steel.' She couldn't help herself. Dammit, she'd suffered beneath the model's poisonous tongue and the scars inflicted had been painfully real. Too real, for they still stung. 'What reason did she give for needing you at her side? A stint in rehab?' She was on a roll. 'An offer you couldn't refuse?'

'Mette was diagnosed with a malignant inoperable brain tumour a week after you walked out.' He spared her a long contemplative look. 'As you know, there's a lifelong connection between her family and mine.' He paused in reflection. 'My mother needed my support for a time. I also had to oversee my father's extensive business interests. A request to hospital-visit Mette each week during that time didn't appear unreasonable.' He paused, then added quietly, 'I accompanied Mother to Mette's funeral last week.' Within thirty-six hours he had been aboard his private jet to Melbourne.

It explained why Mette had disappeared from the European catwalks and the social pages. 'She loved you.' Was obsessed by you, Lianne added silently. To the point where she would have done anything, hurt anyone, in her bid to claim you as her own.

Tyler's gaze didn't waver. 'I didn't love her. At no time did I give Mette any indication we could be anything but friends.'

He wouldn't have had to, Lianne reflected silently. He possessed an inherent male presence that meshed intense sensuality with an animalistic sense of power. Add charm, a hint of leashed savagery, and the effect was dramatic and incredibly potent.

Women coveted his attention, some more blatantly than others, but none were so determined as Mette had been.

'So you said at the time.' She retained a vivid memory of the accusations she'd flung at him, the angry words, and his denial.

'You could, *should*, have trusted me,' he chastised with deceptive mildness.

'We've already done this.'

'In anger,' Tyler agreed. 'I'd like to run it through again. This time—'

'With truth, and rationale?' Lianne posed carefully.

'I can't stop you from trying.'

He replaced his cutlery and pushed his plate aside before leaning back in his chair, his expression contemplative as he regarded her. 'Mette really did a number on you.' There was a degree of wry resignation apparent.

Lianne forked the last morsel of food on her plate and followed it with a sip of wine, then she carefully replaced the goblet on the table. 'Am I supposed to thank you for acknowledging it?'

The pain was still there. He caught a glimpse of it in the thudding pulse at the base of her throat, the careful way she swallowed the wine.

'Unfortunately, I had no control over what she chose to say to you.'

And Mette had said plenty. Even now, the bitter words echoed inside Lianne's head. Instant recall, and not one word missed.

'She was very convincing.' *Extremely* so...to the point where it fell into the Oscar acting category.

'Without any basis,' Tyler assured.

'I have only your word on that.'

The waiter appeared, topped up their goblets, removed their plates and retreated.

'Which you choose not to believe.'

She met his gaze and held it, trying to read something from his expression and failing miserably. 'You expect too much.'

'I had hoped what we shared was worth fighting for.'

'Oh, I fought, Tyler. Hard and long during our marriage.' A *year*, dammit! 'I won a few battles, but in the end Mette won the war.' She drew in a deep breath. 'Now, are we done?'

'Not yet.'

'I am.' She stood and turned to leave, except his

hand snaked out and caught hers before she could take a step.

'Sit down.'

Lianne glared at him. 'Let me go.'

'Not in this lifetime.' His voice was pure steel.

'Tyler—' She tried to wrench her hand free without success. 'There's no purpose to any of this.'

'We can discuss it here, in the car, the apartment,' he said silkily. 'Your choice.'

Lianne recalled the letter she had written to him, stating she had no intention of returning to New York in the near future. She had acquired an unlisted phone number and had all her cellphone calls go to the message bank.

'Your main,' a voice intruded, and Lianne became aware of the waiter's presence.

'Is everything to your satisfaction? Would you prefer I hold the meal?'

'Everything's fine,' Lianne assured as she tugged her hand free. 'Unfortunately I need to leave.'

'We both do,' Tyler informed him smoothly. It took only seconds to retrieve a few notes from his wallet, more than enough to cover the meal, the wine, and provide a sizeable tip. Lianne managed to get as far as the door before he joined her.

She was a piece of work. He wanted to shake her, then kiss her senseless. Preferably here, now. So help him, he would if she so much as opened her mouth.

'Where do you think you're going?'

'Home,' Lianne declared succinctly. She shot him a dark glance that lost much of its heat beneath the shadowy lighting.

'My car is parked in the opposite direction,' Tyler drawled.

She spotted a cruising taxi and hailed it, watching with satisfaction as it drew in to the kerb. 'Goodnight.' She reached for the door, only to have strong fingers close over her wrist.

'Oh, no, you don't.' The voice was silkily quiet close to her ear, and in one fluid movement Tyler opened the front passenger door, offered an apology, then despatched the driver on his way.

'You had no right—'

'Wrong.' His fingers threaded her own and tightened measurably when she attempted to pull free.

Lianne gritted her teeth. 'Fine.' And dug her nails into his knuckles *hard*.

'You want to play this out in public?' Tyler's query was deceptively mild as he turned towards her.

She tilted her chin. 'Not *anywhere*.'

Smart, sassy, courageous…and stubborn as all get out. 'Pity,' he drawled. Without warning he shifted his hands to her shoulders and lowered his head, claiming her mouth with his own before she had a chance to resist.

Drowning would be an apt description as she felt her knees buckle, and she leaned in as one hand fisted her hair while the other slid to the base of her spine, holding her there as he plundered her mouth.

It was all heat, fire and passion as he took her to the brink, fought her resistance and won.

A faint moan rose in her throat, and hands that had beat against his broad back moments before unclenched and slid up to link at his nape.

Magic. Mesmeric. Emotions swirled through her body and swept her high to a place where there was no room for thought. Only the meshing of something wild and primitive with a need for more...much more.

Lianne uttered a silent groan as she felt the potent hardness of his arousal pressing evocatively against her belly, the heavy sensual heat encompassing them both, and with it the unbearable desire to feel skin against skin.

He had the power to make her forget who she was...there was only him, and the electrifying witchery of raw desire.

Lianne had no idea how long they stood completely absorbed in each other. She only knew she didn't want it to end, and she gave a murmur of protest as he began to soften the kiss, lingered gently, then lightly brushed her lips before raising his head.

The raucous sound of a car horn and a male voice shouting, 'Get a room,' brought a stark return to reality.

Hell, necking in plain sight on a public street wasn't something she'd foolishly indulged in since her teens! Where was her sanity?

'That was despicable,' Lianne managed shakily as she pulled away from him.

'The interruption?' Tyler's drawling voice held teasing amusement, and she reacted without thought as she aimed a fist at his shoulder.

He chose not to feint it, nor did he make a move to stop her as she hailed a taxi travelling in the opposite direction.

Instead he watched the vehicle perform a sweeping

turn and pull into the kerb, collect Lianne, then move swiftly down the long stretch that was Toorak Road.

He could afford to let her go. Just as he'd been affected by what they'd just shared...so had she. And there was a sense of satisfaction in the knowledge.

Tyler stood for a minute watching the bright tail-lights disappear, then he turned and walked the short distance to his car.

Minutes later he slid in behind the wheel and fired the engine, then he sent the vehicle purring towards Brighton, heard the buzz of his cellphone and swung in to park kerb-side.

An international call, which precipitated another, then when he was done he cruised until he found a café, parked close by, and enjoyed the Italian-style ambience whilst indulging in a plate of seafood pasta. Not that food was a high priority, but a bouquet starter in an upmarket restaurant didn't come close to comprising a satisfactory meal.

Lianne paid off the driver as soon as the taxi slid to a halt outside the entrance to her apartment block, and it took only seconds to clear security and summon a lift.

Fool. Cool, calm and collected, huh? Show Tyler she was over him and moving on with her life?

Yeah, *sure*. She'd *melted* out there. Right down to a stupid puddle. *His*, for the taking. And he'd taken.

Worse, was her response.

A groan in self-castigation didn't come close to expressing how she felt as she unlocked her apartment and flipped the light switch.

The quiet solitude didn't ease the feeling of helpless frustration as she entered the kitchen, filched bottled water from the refrigerator and took a long swallow.

It would have been infinitely more beneficial to pour herself a shot of whiskey and take it down in one gulp. Alcohol would dull the edges, but nothing…*nothing* would take away the memory of the kiss they'd shared a short while ago.

Tyler had managed to reach down and caress her soul. Her body still sang from his touch, her lips were swollen and she could taste his mouth, *feel* the way it had possessed her own.

He was as much a part of her as she was of him. Worse, he seemed bent on proving it to her by being constantly in her face. Just as she was intent on refusing to acknowledge that what had once existed between them was as alive and well now as it had been from the outset.

Lianne carried the bottled water into the lounge and stood at the set of wide glass doors giving view to the dark ocean waters.

Reflected light from various homes, apartment buildings and street lamps stood out against the backdrop of star-studded skies above, and she stared sightlessly out towards the horizon as she assessed the evening.

News of Blair Benedict's sudden death had been shattering. So too, to a lesser degree, had been Mette's terminal illness. Each of which had gone unnoticed by the Australian media.

If she'd taken one of Tyler's calls…would it have made a difference? Changed her perspective?

Honesty compelled her to admit she didn't know.

Lianne turned away and walked down the hallway. It wasn't late but she coveted the sanctuary of her bedroom, and the possibility of facing Tyler again tonight was more than she could bear.

A brief penned note on the kitchen servery greeted Lianne the next morning.

In Sydney until Friday. Tyler.

He'd added his cellphone number.

Strategy or genuine business interests? Whatever… it provided a welcome respite, and she turned up the car stereo a little louder as she drove into the city.

Michael Sloane senior assigned various title searches, together with pending agreements for perusal and several phone calls to make on his behalf, a few internet searches and notations…all of which took her well into the late afternoon and the day's conference call.

'My wife is a committee member of a few charity organizations,' Michael senior voiced as she prepared to leave his office.

Lianne gave him her interested attention. 'How nice for her.' *Nice?* Surely she could have come up with a better superlative?

'There's a major fund-raiser on Saturday evening,' he informed, sending her a studied look. 'As Tyler Benedict is new in town I've invited him to join our table.' He paused. 'He suggested you as a suitable partner.'

No. The denial was a silent scream. *Don't do this to me.*

'I'd consider it a tremendous favour if you'll agree to accompany him.'

She had to hand it to Tyler…he was *good*. And devious, having Michael senior issue the suggestion, knowing full well she'd refuse if he extended the invitation himself.

'It will be a pleasure,' Lianne accepted politely, whilst mentally planning to verbally castigate Tyler at the first opportunity. 'You'll furnish details? Venue, time, meeting point?'

Michael senior inclined his head. 'Of course. I appreciate you giving up your evening.'

She merely smiled in response.

Lianne joined the general exodus leaving the office at five, and she walked two blocks to the restaurant where she was due to meet Zoe for an evening meal before taking in a movie.

Light relief, she accorded as she threaded her way past several tables to where Zoe was already seated.

Tall, with classic features, liquid brown eyes, a mobile mouth and long sable hair, Zoe had been her closest friend since forever. They'd shared boarding school, puberty…sisters in every way except name.

'Now, tell me why Tyler was in your apartment last night.'

'No *hello* first?' Lianne teased and met Zoe's sparkling gaze.

'Hi,' Zoe responded obediently. 'How are you? Now *tell*, before I expire from curiosity.'

She did, briefly, and glimpsed Zoe's concern.

'This is OK with you?'

Not OK at all, for all the obvious reasons. 'His apartment, his building. He's merely using a room to sleep in...not *mine*,' she assured. 'While he's in Melbourne.'

'And you believe that?'

'About as much as you do.'

'So, what's the plan?'

Lianne effected an expressive eye-roll. 'To stay out of his way as much as possible.'

'Interesting.' And difficult, Zoe determined silently, convinced Tyler had a different agenda in mind.

They ordered a light meal, followed it with coffee, then they crossed to the cinema-plex, bought tickets and viewed the current multi-Oscar nominated movie. Afterwards they lingered over coffee and bade each other goodnight.

'Take care,' Zoe offered with genuine sincerity, and Lianne reciprocated,

'You, too.'

The weekend loomed, with no sign of Tyler. The slim hope Lianne held that he might not return in time for the Charity Benefit was dashed when she re-entered the apartment on Saturday morning after a punishing session at the gym to find him in the kitchen fixing coffee.

She was suddenly conscious of the way she looked. She felt a mess, her hair was damp from her exertion, her sweats clung, and her priority was a shower and change of clothes.

His dark grey eyes speared hers and she hated the

familiar curling sensation in her stomach, the increased pulse-beat, at the sight of him.

It was almost as if her body recognised his on some base level and immediately went on to full alert.

It wasn't a feeling she coveted or liked, and she silently damned him for his determination to turn her life upside down.

'Good morning.'

His faint mocking smile was her undoing and she launched directly into attack mode.

'Just what do you mean by having Michael Sloane senior act as your intermediary?'

Tyler leant back against the servery and regarded her steadily. 'Whatever happened to ''hello''?' When she didn't deign to answer he queried, 'Specifically in reference to?'

'Don't play with me,' she warned. *'Tonight.'*

'Ah,' he acknowledged in a silky drawl. 'The Charity Benefit.'

'That's the one.'

'You object?'

Lianne fluttered her eyelashes in mock parody. 'Why, I'm absolutely thrilled and delighted. Partnering you is a dream come true.' She dropped the pose. 'Of course I object,' she said fiercely. 'What made you think I wouldn't?'

'Deal with it.'

She wanted to hit him, and almost gave in to the temptation. Except he'd never let her get away with it. The silent threat was there in his stance, his expression.

'It's my day for cleaning the apartment and doing the week's grocery shopping,' she said stiffly.

'So...keep out of your way?'

'Yes!'

'Got it in one.'

It said much that he left the apartment soon after and didn't return until late afternoon.

CHAPTER FIVE

LIANNE fixed one ear-stud, then dealt with the other.

The gown she'd chosen to wear was champagne silk chiffon with a fitted beaded top, spaghetti straps and a skirt that fell in soft folds to her feet. A matching silk beaded wrap added an elegant finishing touch, together with stiletto-heeled pumps.

The length of her hair was caught into a smooth chignon, and her make-up was understated with emphasis on her eyes.

Her nervousness had little to do with a lack of self-esteem or low self-confidence. Nor did the prospect of joining Michael Sloane senior and his son as their invited guest at the evening's charity benefit.

A glittering fund-raiser, the guest list had to be impressive, with society matrons endeavouring to outdo each other whilst adopting the personae of maintaining pseudo friendships, and men in splendid tailoring portraying practised conviviality.

It wasn't the event or the guests, she admittedly wryly. Just *one* guest, invited to share the same table and with whom she'd be expected to indulge in polite conversation during the evening.

Lianne took a deep breath and slowly released it, then she caught up her evening purse and made her way to the lounge.

Tyler was standing at the wide expanse of plate glass, seemingly intent on observing the view.

He turned as she entered the room and she was struck by the look of him, his impeccable tailoring and the sheer power he exuded.

'Beautiful,' he complimented, and she summoned a dazzling smile as she inclined her head.

'Thank you.'

Act. It really wasn't too hard. Just smile a lot and laugh occasionally.

'I think we should arrive separately at the hotel venue,' Lianne declared and incurred his musing smile.

'Your reason being?'

'You're the auspicious client and honoured guest,' she managed solemnly. 'I'm part of the firm.'

'That makes a difference…because?'

A slight frown creased her forehead. 'If we appear together it might give the wrong impression.'

Tyler moved towards her. 'And that would be such a bad thing?'

She affected him as no other woman had…or could, he admitted silently. She was his light, his life, everything. If he could turn back the clock…

He'd thought what they shared was strong enough to withstand any interference. It didn't sit well having to admit he'd miscalculated the effect Mette's devious meddling would have, or that Lianne had imagined her only option was to flee.

'I'm sure, in the interests of Sloane, Everton, Shell and Associates, it would be preferable for the staff to maintain a professional relationship with the clientele.'

A faint smile tugged the corners of his mouth. 'The exception being if one of the staff happens to be married to one of the clientele?'

He watched her eyes widen and begin to cloud. 'We're separated. Estranged,' she qualified. 'I'm filing for divorce.'

Tyler lifted a hand and brushed gentle fingers across her cheek. 'So adamant.' He wanted, *needed* to make love to her until every last vestige of doubt in her mind was removed.

Except trust required time to repair and restore. And he had all the time in the world. He'd made sure of it.

He dropped his hand and caught up his keys. 'Shall we leave?'

'I'm taking my car.'

'If that's what you prefer.'

'You can take yours.'

He shot her a steady look. 'We go together.'

'What if we each want to leave the venue at different times?'

'We compromise.'

'With different partners,' Lianne persisted, just for the hell of it, and saw his eyes narrow.

'You want to argue?' His drawled query was dangerously silky.

'Endorse my independence,' she qualified as she moved towards the door.

'Proving?'

She gained the bank of lifts and pressed the call button, aware he was only a step behind her. 'That I can,' she managed sweetly, and heard his soft laughter as he followed her into the lift.

They took the Porsche with Tyler at the wheel, obtained valet parking at the hotel venue, and entered the foyer together.

The grand ballroom was situated on the first floor, surrounded by balconies, reached by a wide curving staircase, and a quick glance revealed that numerous guests were already assembled on the spacious balconies.

Smile-time, Lianne accorded silently as she gained the upper floor and accepted a flute of champagne from one of several hovering waiters.

It was mildly amusing to witness the interest Tyler's presence achieved. While some of it was covert, a number of women displayed a marked lack of reticence, whilst two of the city's well-known society doyennes…the noted Pamela Whitcroft and her arch enemy, Eleanora Postlewaite…conducted a mental race as to whom would claim him first.

'It's your fatal charm,' Lianne accorded several minutes later when both women melted back into the crowd. 'Be assured your name will now appear on all the most prestigious guest lists in town.'

'Indeed?'

She offered him a winsome smile. 'You doubt it?'

'I lend my support to numerous charities.'

'Watch and observe. Before night's end, your little black book will be filled.'

He leaned in close. 'What little black book?'

'The one you'll need to keep track.'

'Maybe you should consider acquiring one of your own.'

'Why?'

His smile deepened. 'I'll require a partner.'

'It won't be me.'

'Count on it.'

'Tyler,' a familiar male voice intruded. 'I see you've caught up with Lianne.'

Lianne turned towards Michael Sloane senior and offered a polite greeting, while Tyler inclined his head.

'You must allow me to introduce you to a few friends and associates.'

Prominent members of the city's social echelon, she perceived, recognising a few people who regularly graced the social pages of newspapers and trade magazines.

Six-thirty for eight allowed more than an hour to mix and mingle with fellow guests, sip a glass or two or three of champagne and nibble on canapés.

She'd had plenty of practice playing the social game during her year in New York as Tyler's wife. The beautiful people who judged and were judged by the size of their home, its location, the cars they owned, how often they travelled and where, the wife's jewellery, complement of servants, homes abroad, and the size of their wallets.

By comparison, tonight's soirée should be a cinch.

'My apologies,' Michael junior declared as he joined them. 'I was unavoidably detained.'

Michael senior effected the introduction, then turned towards her. 'Lianne. You'll excuse us?'

'Of course.'

'So that's wonder-boy,' Michael junior commented quietly as soon as Tyler moved away with his father. 'What's your reaction?'

Oh, my. You really don't want to know! 'Tyler Benedict?'

'Who else?' His eyes narrowed. 'You're prevaricating. Why?'

'Too rich, too attractive. Too much,' Lianne accorded with deliberate indolence. 'Will that do?'

He looked thoughtful. 'Hmm. Got to you, didn't he?'

She arched one eyebrow and incurred his cynical smile.

'Too many *toos*,' he relayed, deadpan.

'Perhaps we should mingle. It's expected, don't you think?'

'Walk the talk? Why not?' He flashed her a brilliant smile. 'We'll begin with my mother.'

The woman behind the man? Subservient or society matron?

Society, definitely, Lianne perceived. Old money, well versed in the social graces, and a mother who demanded only the very best for her son.

It was oh so carefully done, with gentle queries, expressed warmth…but Lianne had the impression she was being analysed, dissected and probed with a view to her suitability to consort with the junior male Sloane.

'Incredible, isn't she?' Michael junior murmured as they moved away.

'I'd have said *formidable*.'

His quiet laughter appeared genuine. 'What do I have to do to keep you in my life?'

'Please take note...I'm not *in* your life.'

'Not yet.'

'Do you ever give up?'

'I'm known for my tenacity,' he declared solemnly and draped a friendly arm around her waist. 'Didn't you know?'

'What works in the courtroom isn't necessarily effective out of it.'

'Wisdom is such an admirable trait.'

She offered him a stunning smile and stepped away. 'Isn't it just?'

At that moment she had the unnerving sensation she was being watched. With care she idly skimmed the crowd, pausing when she sighted a familiar dark head.

Tyler, whose indolent dark gaze speared hers for a few heart-stopping seconds before he returned his attention to the man at his side.

Lianne's stomach executed a slow curl, settled fractionally, and it was perhaps as well the wide double doors leading in to the ballroom swung open and staff began encouraging the guests to take their seats.

Round tables, white linen, sparkling silver and glassware, elegant table decorations and piped background music.

'Second table to the right, centre upfront,' Michael junior instructed as he urged her to precede him.

The tickets had to be expensive. Make that very expensive, she mused as she noted prominent Australian wines gracing the tables.

Michael Sloane senior had nominated himself in

charge of seating arrangements, and Lianne found herself manoeuvred neatly between Tyler and Michael junior.

It was crazy to be conscious of every breath she took, *aware*, as if her body recognised Tyler on a base level.

Oh, who was she kidding?

Just go with the flow. Sip some wine, eat a little. Converse. How hard could it be?

'You have a conquest,' Tyler commented quietly, and she cast him a steady look.

'You think?'

'Don't milk it.'

She offered a polite smile. 'Now why would I do that?'

'To irritate me?'

The smile widened. 'Is it working?'

'Just remember I get to take you home.'

Lianne turned her attention to the wine steward tending their table, and when he was done she reached for her water glass.

'Is our honoured guest hitting on you?'

She met Michael junior's steady gaze and her mouth curved a little. 'What makes you think that?'

'Because you're hot. And he's interested.'

'Am I supposed to be overwhelmed?'

His eyes speared hers. 'Are you?'

You don't know the half of it! 'I've no desire to have a man complicate my life,' she responded lightly, and took a sip from her glass.

'Maybe I can change your mind.'

Not in a million years, Lianne assured silently as

she offered a suitably innocuous smile. Been there, done that, and don't aim to do it again.

It was a relief as the lights dimmed and the charity chairperson took the podium, enlightening the guests on the fund-raiser's purpose, and requesting they give generously for a worthy cause.

After which the MC announced the evening's entertainment and a line of waiters began serving the starter.

Social conversation was an acquired skill and Lianne's fellow table guests were well-versed in the art.

Tyler's presence proved a distraction, and Lianne dealt with the fine body heat simmering beneath the surface, acutely conscious of his close proximity, the faint aroma of his cologne…her favoured Cerruti, which caused her to wonder if it had been a deliberate choice.

It revived memories of similar events in another city on the other side of the world. Occasions when the only cloud on her horizon had been Mette's intrusion and the model's subtle taunts that *she* was Lianne's predecessor in Tyler's bed. One of many, Mette had implied, not averse to hinting that Tyler still sought her on occasion, delighting in her revelations causing Lianne emotional pain.

'Lianne. More wine?'

She dispensed the image and met Tyler's dark enigmatic gaze. 'No. Thanks,' she added with a polite smile, and felt her pulse quicken to a faster beat.

Had he sensed her train of thought? It was an uncanny ability he'd acquired early in their relationship, and had rarely ceased to surprise her.

Did he know tonight's social affair was the first she'd attended since she left New York? And to appear *with* him presented her with a sensation of *déjà vu*?

It wasn't something she wanted, for she'd put the past behind her and moved on. *Hadn't she?*

A tiny bubble of laughter rose and died in her throat. *As if.*

There was an entertainment segment between courses and the food presentation was a masterpiece in culinary expertise.

Although Lianne's tastebuds appeared to have gone on strike as she forked minute morsels into her mouth between alternate sips of water and wine.

Throughout the evening she conversed with every guest at the table, smiled until her facial muscles began to ache and, without meaning to, gave Michael junior more attention than was warranted.

Tyler found it easy to maintain an expected façade. He was adept at projecting an image and sufficiently knowledgeable to discuss any topic a fellow guest chose to explore.

It was interesting to watch the social play, to speculate what lay beneath the surface of each and every guest seated at the table.

Michael Sloane senior portrayed a certain degree of satisfaction that he'd scored a high profile client as a guest, while his wife was a society doyenne *par excellence*.

Michael junior showed too much interest in Lianne. Something which alternately amused and irritated him. Lianne hadn't dated, that much was clear from weekly reports despatched to his New York office.

If there was anything between them it had been confined to work hours. And possibly one-sided. The thought it might not be caused his stomach muscles to tighten.

Only for the sensation to relax and move lower and settle uncomfortably in the region of his groin.

The way she'd responded to him hadn't been contrived. No one could accelerate their own heartbeat or fake sensual heat. When he'd kissed her she'd been there with him all the way. *His* for the taking. And he almost had…except it wouldn't have resolved anything other than sexual lust.

He wasn't fool enough to think otherwise.

Countless times he'd damned Mette's obsessive behaviour. God knew he hadn't given her any cause to think there was anything other than friendship between them.

He, who imagined he *knew* women, hadn't sensed that Mette might have assumed another persona…one that bordered close to delusion. He could deal with anything directed at himself. Lianne was something else.

A muscle bunched momentarily at the edge of his jaw. To have Lianne choose to abandon the marriage and retreat had surprised and angered him.

Afterwards he'd cursed fate for the hand it played him. His father's accidental death. Family responsibilities, priorities. Mette's illness.

It had taken valuable time. Too much, he perceived wryly. Lianne's letter to him in New York citing her intention to file for divorce had reached him via email within hours of his arrival in Melbourne.

Fear and anger had meshed into something he'd fought to control. It was then he had changed his mind about booking into a hotel. Instead he'd taken a cab to Lianne's apartment and claimed temporary residence.

This time she wouldn't escape. He'd make sure of it.

'Tyler,' a soft feminine voice intruded, accompanied by a light laugh. 'A business deal, or is it a woman?'

He had to think to recall her name as he turned towards the woman seated opposite him. Becky? Belinda?

'Does it have to be one or the other?'

Her eyes sparkled with an open invitation. 'Perhaps I can help make up your mind?'

His tone was gentle. 'I doubt my wife would approve.'

The luscious mouth formed a pretty pout. 'Does she have to know?'

'I'm flattered.'

'But not interested.'

He merely smiled.

The evening was winding down, coffee had been served, the speeches were done, the entertainment programme complete, Lianne noted with a sense of relief.

'Want to go on to a nightclub?'

Michael junior, ready and eager to party. The thought of a noisy crowd, loud music and standing room only didn't appeal. 'Can I take a raincheck?' It was a cop-out, yet more kind than an outright refusal.

His hand brushed her shoulder. 'Do you need a ride home?'

'Thanks, but I have it covered.'

It was several minutes before Michael Sloane senior and his wife took their leave, which prompted fellow guests at the table to do likewise.

Lianne breathed a mental sigh of relief that the evening was almost at an end. All she had to do was maintain a pleasant smile, murmur a few gracious words as she joined the general exodus from the grand ballroom…and keep a few steps ahead of Tyler.

A fruitless exercise, given he was *there* at her side, his tall frame almost protecting her own as they threaded their way through the crowd.

It was ridiculous to fall prey to a sense of helpless rage. Just as it was foolish to attempt to pretend a wholly professional relationship. What did it matter if it appeared they'd struck a mutual chord?

Who cared?

Except *she* did. And it had everything to do with the need to maintain a distance from the man who'd caused her so much emotional turmoil.

Valet parking provided a delay as uniformed attendants efficiently delivered patrons' vehicles. As fate would have it the Sloanes were positioned behind Tyler in the waiting queue, and Lianne could almost sense their speculation as she slipped into the passenger seat of Tyler's Porsche.

Within seconds he cleared the hotel entrance, entered the stream of traffic negotiating the inner city and headed south towards Brighton.

'It might be as well to enlighten Sloane senior and junior as to your true identity.'

She turned towards him and noted the strong male profile outlined by passing street lights, the angles and planes, the firm jaw. 'Oh, sure. That'll work.' She adopted a professional persona... 'By the way, *Marshall* is my family name. In reality I'm Lianne *Benedict*, your eminent client's soon-to-be ex-wife.' She returned her gaze to the passing scenery beyond the windscreen. 'Whereupon I offer my apologies for the deception, cite a conflict of interest, and tender my resignation.' Without missing a beat she continued, '*Dare* intercede and I'll have to kill you.'

'There's just one thing,' Tyler said in a silky-smooth voice. 'Drop the *soon-to-be ex*.'

Dignified silence was the only way to go, and she maintained it during the short drive home and in the lift. Once inside the apartment she made straight for her bedroom...only to have her progress stopped by firm hands closing over her shoulders.

'Don't,' she warned quickly.

He turned her round to face him and saw her eyes dilate, the tell-tale tension evident in her pale features. And the faint tremble of her mouth.

'Headache?'

His intent gaze was too much, and she closed her eyes against the sight of him.

She felt his hands slide over her shoulders and cup her face, the light brush of his lips to her forehead.

Oh, dear God, don't do this to me, she pleaded silently. She couldn't afford his warmth or the solicitous gentleness he offered.

'Where do you keep medication? Kitchen? Bathroom?'

'Bedroom *en suite*.'

His mouth touched hers, so briefly she almost thought she'd imagined it.

'Go on down. I'll fill a glass with water.'

'I don't need a nurse.' Tension headaches were a curse…and let's face it she'd had more than her share of tension in the few days since Tyler had walked back into her life!

All she wanted was a good night's sleep, aided by two strong painkillers.

Her room was in darkness and she switched on the lamp, dimmed it low, then observed a nightly ritual…cleanse off make-up, teeth, undo her hair, remove her clothes, slip into nightwear.

She was almost done when Tyler entered the room, glass in hand. 'Go away.'

'When you've taken the necessary meds.'

Lianne pulled open a drawer, extracted two tablets from their foil pack, took the glass from his hand and swallowed them down. 'Satisfied?'

She resembled a belligerent child, her face bare, hair pulled back into a ponytail and wearing an oversize T-shirt. He had an urge to sweep her into his arms and tumble her down on to the bed.

'Now there's a question.' The edges of his mouth curved a little. 'Want me to answer it?'

She winced in pain and lifted a hand, then let it fall

helplessly to her side. 'Take your libido and get out of here.'

Tyler bit back an oath and slid her between the bed-covers in one smooth movement. 'Shut up. Close your eyes and sleep.'

'I hate you.'

'Uh-huh.' He turned the light down until the room was shrouded in semi-darkness. 'You need anything in the night...just call.'

'I'd rather die first.'

CHAPTER SIX

SUNDAY dawned bright and clear. Lianne rose early, spent an hour in the gym, then showered and changed into dress jeans and shirt; she added a denim jacket, collected car-keys, her bag, stopped by the kitchen to filch bottled water from the fridge…and almost bumped into Tyler.

He looked far too fit in hip-hugging black jeans and black T-shirt.

Her stomach curled and went into a mini free fall at the sexual energy he seemed to exude without any effort at all.

'Going out?'

His voice affected her every time. Low, husky… *sexy*, in a way no man had a right to be this early on a Sunday morning.

'Yes.'

'*Sans* breakfast?'

Lianne bore his appraisal with equanimity, and managed to lift one eyebrow in silent query.

'I'll pick up something.' Orange juice, latte, a croissant in any one of numerous coffee boutiques where she'd skim the Sunday newspapers before heading into the city.

'Enjoy.'

She offered him a brilliant smile. 'Oh, I shall.'

Then she moved past him, exited the apartment and took the lift down to the basement car park.

There was no clear plan to the day except the need to escape the apartment…and Tyler.

Lianne chose Toorak, parked, then she selected one of several coffee boutiques and spent a pleasurable hour over a light breakfast while she scanned the courtesy newspapers.

From there she headed into the city and conducted some serious retail therapy, took in a movie, enjoyed a Caesar salad that doubled as a late lunch and early evening meal, then she slid into her Mini Cooper and drove to the Brighton apartment.

Tyler's Porsche was there when she pulled into her car space and she gave a faint sigh as she collected her purchases, then took the lift to her level.

Any hope he might be in the gym was dashed when she entered the apartment, for the smell of food tantalised her tastebuds…pasta sauce, she determined, identifying the subtle aroma of tomato, garlic and spices.

Lianne deposited her carrier bags, walked into the kitchen and saw Tyler standing at the cook top stirring the redolent sauce with a wooden spoon.

He turned towards her, offered a warm smile, scooped a small quantity of sauce on to the spoon and held it out to her. 'Try this.'

OK, she could play the game. Without a word she crossed to where he stood, dipped a finger into the spoon and tasted.

'You haven't lost your touch.' As soon as the words left her mouth she wanted to take them back.

The edge of Tyler's mouth twitched with humour, and his gleaming gaze brought a tinge of pink to her cheeks.

'I assume you're referring to food?'

'Naturally. Sex isn't even an issue here.'

He laid down the spoon and leaned one hip against the counter edge. 'Have I tried to seduce you?'

Dammit, he was enjoying this. While she seemed to be getting in deeper with every word she uttered. It was time to try another strategy. 'Are you willing to swear you won't?'

Tyler appeared to give it some thought. 'No.'

Her pulse went into overdrive and she consciously controlled her breathing. 'Try it, and I'll do you a mortal injury.'

He crossed arms over his chest and regarded her with a degree of amused mockery. 'I consider myself warned.'

Straightening, he checked the sauce, turned down the heat, then tested the pasta.

'Are you going to join me?'

'I've already eaten.' The thought of sharing his company and battling her emotions didn't appeal. Hadn't that been why she'd escaped for the day? 'I'm going to spend an hour in the study, then catch an early night.'

Tyler tipped the pasta into a colander, added a knob of butter, and spared her a direct look. 'I'm flying to Cairns early in the morning for a day or two.'

'Have a successful trip.' With that she vacated the kitchen, deposited her carrier bags in the bedroom, and crossed into the study.

It was almost nine when she closed the laptop. She could hear the faint noise of the television and had an image of Tyler seated comfortably viewing one programme or another.

She told herself she didn't care. Reiterated it as she showered, then slipped into bed. At least she could look forward to a forty-eight hour respite from his presence coming up. Not exactly celebration territory, but a small air-punch wouldn't go amiss! Something she effected just for the hell of it.

Nevertheless the apartment seemed strangely empty when she entered the kitchen next morning and found Tyler had already left.

The day became one of *those* days where anything that could go wrong did. It began with a fellow driver cutting in too close at an intersection, and it was only quick action on her part that prevented a collision.

From there on in it went from bad to worse. The assistant Michael senior had assigned her appeared to be suffering a bad hormone day, as each request Lianne issued was met with increasingly visible irritation. Around three o'clock the assistant threw a hissy fit and took the rest of the afternoon off.

An action which left Lianne with extra work to get through. At five she weighed up whether to take work home or stay on.

There was nothing waiting for her at home except a solitary meal, catching up with email, a few phone calls... Besides, there was something satisfying about finishing up the day's work at the office.

An hour and a half, maybe two tops, and she'd be done.

The decision made, she notified Reception, extracted bottled water from the small bar fridge, took a long swallow and settled down in front of the computer.

It was mainly admin work, scanning in data, tying it in seamlessly with Michael senior's cautions and advice in order to compile a comprehensive report that Tyler had requested be emailed through to him in Cairns the following morning.

The mezzanine level seemed a little empty, but she enjoyed the silence, the solitude. Doubtless there were a few legal associates downstairs who'd also chosen to stay back. It wasn't as if she was alone in the firm's suite of offices.

The sudden peal of the phone was unexpected, and a frown creased her forehead as she reached forward to take the call.

'Lianne? Michael. Feel like sharing a coffee break?'

He was working late? Michael junior was known to be first out the door at day's end. His strict adherence to the clock was a bit of a joke among his fellow staff.

'I hadn't planned on a break. Ten, fifteen minutes and I'll be out of here.'

'OK, I'll meet you in the foyer in fifteen.'

The call terminated before she could offer a refusal.

A soft imprecation fell from her lips. On the surface Michael's attention appeared as lighthearted, bantering fun. Yet occasionally she had the impression there was a seriousness beneath it all.

Ten minutes later she closed down the laptop, caught up her bag and headed to Reception. It was almost seven; it had been a long day, and the last thing she felt inclined to do was spend out-of-office time with the head partner's son.

Michael was waiting for her when she reached the foyer, and together they rode the lift down to ground level.

Lianne didn't miss a beat as they reached the external set of doors. 'There's a café at the end of the block.'

'Why not head to Southbank? We can look out over the river, and the food is to die for.'

There it was again, that instinctive, almost intuitive feeling. 'Michael, it's coffee, not a meal.'

He spread his hands in a defensive gesture. 'OK, got it. Coffee.'

It didn't take long to reach the café, and they found an empty table just in from the entrance.

'So,' Michael began after they'd given their order. 'What gives with wonder-boy?'

Lianne lifted an eyebrow. 'I assume you're referring to Tyler Benedict?'

'One and the same.'

She looked at him evenly. 'You must know I can't discuss his business affairs.'

'It's the personal angle I'm interested in.'

'Is that why you invited me to share coffee?'

'Is it such a crime to want to spend time with you?'

'Michael,' she protested. 'We're legal colleagues. That's all.'

'What if I want more?'

'But I don't,' she managed quietly.

'Are you going to insult me with the *it's not you, it's me* spiel?'

'No.'

A waitress presented their coffee, then moved on to take an order from another table.

Lianne added one sugar and stirred the aromatic brew.

It was hot, and she sipped carefully, wanting only to drink it as quickly as possible and leave.

'Who is he?'

'I'm sorry?'

'The man in your life.'

This was getting tiresome. She looked at him steadily. 'I don't have one.'

'So…why not me?'

'Friends and colleagues.' She effected a light shrug. 'That's as far as it goes,' she declared firmly.

'Tell me what I have to do to change your mind.'

Lianne had had enough. 'Nothing. Absolutely nothing.' With one smooth movement she stood, extracted a note and placed it beneath her cup. Then she turned and walked out of the café.

She banked down irritation during the short distance to the office basement car park and, although it wasn't intentional, there was a certain satisfaction in hearing the noise of squealing tyres as she turned sharply on to the ramp leading to street level.

Her irritation with Michael junior hadn't cooled overmuch when she reached her apartment, and she slipped off her jacket, stepped out of her stilettos and crossed to the kitchen. Food was the furthest thing from her mind, but a long cool drink would suffice, then she'd shower, slip into something comfortable and lose herself in a good book.

Half an hour later she emerged from the shower. Then, dry, she pulled on an oversize T-shirt and wound a towel, turban-style, over her wet hair.

Better, she admitted. The warm, pulsing water had soothed the rough edges and cooled her temper.

Hunger ensured she fixed herself something to eat. Then, just as she was about to call Zoe, her cellphone rang.

'Will you accept an abject apology?'

Something twisted inside her stomach at the sound of Michael junior's voice. 'I'd prefer any conversation between us to be limited to office hours.'

'I'm sorry.'

'Goodnight.' She ended the call and prowled the lounge, only to tense as her cellphone began an insistent peal. If it was Michael junior...

'Lianne.'

Chris. Thank heavens. 'Hi, bro.' Her voice held affectionate warmth. 'Are you OK?'

'Mom just phoned. They're driving up from Geelong Sunday morning for a week or so. Thought we'd plan a barbecue. You'll be here?'

'Of course. I'll bring dessert.'

'Around eleven?'

'Got it. How's Sharon, and Shantel?'

'Fine. We're just not getting much sleep.'

New parents, new babe. She could hear Shantel's distressed crying in the background. 'Go be a good papa.' She smiled at the thought of her brother in the parental role. 'See you Sunday.'

Her niece was a delight, so tiny and perfect. A true

joy for her doting parents. Lianne adored being an aunt.

It was after ten when she went to bed, and late when she closed the book and switched off the lamp.

To her surprise she fell asleep almost at once, and didn't wake until six when the alarm went off.

Half an hour in the gym was followed by a shower, then breakfast, and she was halfway through dressing when her cellphone rang.

'Tyler.' The familiar drawl held a certain brusqueness and she envisaged him checking the day's schedule and making notes as he dealt with each written task. 'I've tied things up here and will be in Melbourne around midday. Will you alert Michael and arrange an early afternoon appointment? SMS me when you have a time.'

'OK.'

'Good morning to you, too,' he offered with musing humour, and cut the call.

Work took Lianne's attention, with a few minor amendments to the report she'd prepared for Michael senior's approval.

It appeared Tyler had several properties in Queensland under consideration, ranging from the Gold Coast to Port Douglas in the north. Vaguely surprising were the inclusion of a few residential homes.

She emailed the report through, printed out triplicate copies, and was about to take a coffee break when an assistant from Reception delivered a stunning floral arrangement.

'For me?' There had to be some mistake.

'I know of only one Lianne Marshall in the firm,'

the attractive assistant assured with a friendly smile. 'I'll organise a vase.'

Who? Her birthday was months away, there was nothing to warrant a congratulatory bouquet…

She plucked the small envelope from its nesting place, extracted the card, read the words and experienced a momentary feeling of unease.

Michael junior. The written message *for you* was innocuous.

An apology? She keyed him a *thanks* text message in acknowledgement, then she checked her day's schedule.

There were phone calls she needed to make, a title search to organise, and enough paperwork to carry her through the day.

Tyler's presence mid-afternoon moved Lianne's nervous tension up a notch, and it took concentrated effort to present a calm persona during the meeting.

If she had thought her participation would be minimal she was mistaken, for Tyler drew her into the discussion as he requested her input on the properties he'd selected as warranting his interest.

'Capital growth on the Gold Coast is at an all-time high on beachfront property,' Lianne opined. She had a knowledge of the area and she'd studied the latest real estate trends. 'Particularly Hedges Avenue at Mermaid Beach. Apartment living is very popular at Main Beach. Both areas have easy access to beaches, trendy society cafés and shopping centres. When it comes to canal-front homes, there are several prestigious areas, with Sovereign Islands numbering high on the list.'

Tyler gave her his total attention. 'And country living?'

'Terranora Heights, Tallai,' she ventured. 'Depending on your definition of *country*. Small or large acreage, remote or with easy access to the main highway north and south.'

'Industrial?'

He was far too astute not to have done his homework. 'It would depend on your purpose.'

He inclined his head. 'Port Douglas?'

'Beachfront,' Lianne said without hesitation. 'Land is at a premium. Existing homes and cottages are being bought and demolished. Low-rise holiday apartments are in demand to cater to the tourist industry.'

'It would be advantageous to have your personal input onsite.' Tyler turned towards Michael senior. 'I trust you'd have no objection?'

Hang on a minute…personal input *onsite*?

'Not at all. When do you envisage this taking place?'

'It'll require two days. Friday? I'll arrange an early morning departure.'

Michael senior appeared to hesitate. 'I had hoped Lianne would join senior members of the firm at a legal soirée held in the city Friday evening.'

'Sounds interesting.'

'Each member is invited to bring a guest. We'd be honoured to have you attend.'

'Thank you.'

Lianne barely refrained from gritting her teeth.

'In that case, the weekend?' Tyler posed. 'Naturally

Lianne will be financially compensated for giving up her free time,' he continued steadily.

Michael senior turned towards Lianne. 'Is this convenient?'

As if she didn't have a life! 'I have plans to spend the day with my family on Sunday.'

Tyler's gaze sharpened, although his voice retained its calm drawling tone. 'I can ensure you're in Melbourne early Sunday afternoon.'

Michael senior beamed. 'Lianne?'

Oh, Lord. 'I'm sure an agent familiar with each area will be able to provide adequate assistance.' It was a last-ditch effort and she knew it.

'I don't want professional opinion based on the size of an agent's commission,' Tyler responded smoothly.

Michael senior's expression hardened slightly in a visual reminder of her recent promotion and expected duties. Which presumably were meant to cater to the eminent client's wishes.

She offered a faint smile in capitulation. 'In that case I'll await confirmation of your departure time.'

'I've also selected two properties here. One in Toorak, the other at Mount Eliza, both of which require a woman's opinion. Shall we say Tuesday morning?'

'Of course.' Michael senior beamed. 'Lianne will be at your disposal for the morning.'

Would she, indeed? Maybe she'd call in sick!

'Lianne?' Tyler's voice was a silky drawl.

'Naturally.' Did either man detect her use of subtle cynicism? Apparently not.

There wasn't anything else she could add within

Michael senior's hearing. However, give her some private time with Tyler, and sparks would fly!

It was almost five when the meeting concluded and, given Michael senior's parting words... 'Lianne will accompany you to Reception,' she had no other recourse but to do just that.

Polite...she could do *polite*. People skills formed an integral part of client relations.

'It appears your trip was successful.'

Tyler shot her a faintly amused glance. 'Indeed.'

'One imagines your Australian sojourn will be relatively short?'

'Not necessarily. In today's electronic age distance has little relevance.'

'Of course.' They reached Reception, where she noticed the practised smiles of the girls manning the front desk reached a brilliance previously unseen.

It didn't help that Michael junior came into view as she extended client courtesy and summoned a lift.

Within a matter of seconds the doors opened, and Tyler did the unexpected by extending his hand. 'Until later.'

Reflex action was responsible for her placing her hand in his. The contact was brief, but electric, then he stepped into the cubicle and hit the ground level button.

Lianne's relief was palpable as she turned and re-entered Reception, although it was short-lived as she caught a glimpse of Michael junior's hurt expression before it was quickly masked.

There was a short debriefing in Michael senior's office, then she returned to her own, shut down the laptop, scooped up the flowers her assistant had thoughtfully wrapped in protective cellophane, caught up her bag and went out to summon the lift.

The hope that she'd be the sole occupant went unfounded, for just as the doors began to close an arm shot through and stalled the action just as she hit the appropriate button.

'Phew. Just made it.'

Michael junior. Coincidence or design?

He indicated the flowers. 'A token atonement to add to my apology. I was way out of line.'

Lianne spared him a direct look. 'Yes, you were.'

'Truce?'

The lift paused and two people joined them, making it easy for her to lapse into silence. They emerged at ground level, while Lianne hit the button for basement level two where her car was parked.

'Truce,' she agreed with a friendly smile.

She moved swiftly towards the row where she'd parked her car, de-sensitised the alarm and felt a hand close over her upper arm.

'Please.'

Lianne stilled and forced her voice into calm, rational tones as she held his gaze. 'Michael. Don't—'

He released her arm and held up both hands palm upwards in a defensive gesture. 'OK. Got it. You don't like anyone invading your personal space.'

'Thank you.' Without a further word she moved towards her car, unlocked the door and slid in behind the wheel, then she fired the engine.

It was almost seven when she entered the apartment, and it took only seconds to realise she wasn't alone.

Food, she could smell food. And there was background music on low, filtering through the speaker system.

The dining room table was set for two. An opened bottle of red wine sat breathing, there was a salad ready to be tossed and the smell of warm bread heating in the oven.

'You're home.'

Tyler appeared in the aperture, looking the antithesis of the high-powered businessman of a few hours ago. The suit was gone, and in its place were hip-hugging jeans and a black fitted T-shirt that hugged every muscle. A tea towel was draped over one shoulder, and he looked…incredible.

Sexy, she admitted. The quintessential sensual male.

'I won't even ask what you're doing,' Lianne said quietly as she stepped out of her stilettos. 'Just give me five minutes to change and pour me a glass of wine.'

His eyes sharpened beneath the indolent smile. 'That bad, huh?'

'In spades,' she acknowledged simply, and bent down to retrieve her shoes. Without a further word she turned and walked down to her bedroom, removed her suit, tights, cleansed her face of make-up and loosened her hair. Then she stepped into jeans, added a T-shirt, and went out to the kitchen.

She looked about sixteen, Tyler observed, and way too pale for his liking.

'Tough day?' he queried lightly as he handed her a glass of wine. 'Missed lunch?'

'Yes, and no.'

'So...' he drawled. 'Want to share?'

She gave him a direct look. 'Not particularly.' She took an appreciative sip of wine, savoured it, and watched as he set two peppered steaks into a sizzling pan.

'Who nominated you as cook?'

'I collected a few provisions, figured you'd soon be home, and decided to make enough for two.'

She reached out, plucked up a potato wedge and popped it into her mouth.

He turned the steaks, waited a bit, then placed one on each plate. 'Go sit down.'

Lianne took her wine, collected the bowl of wedges and crossed to the table, added dressing to the salad and tossed it.

'I'm trying hard to be angry with you.'

He set down each plate. 'Because?'

She threw him an exasperated look. 'Don't toy with me, Tyler. The weekend jaunt,' she elaborated as she took a chair opposite him.

'Ah.' He took a seat and proceeded to serve her a portion of salad before taking a liberal serving for himself.

'Is that all you can say?'

His gaze held a measured quality as he studied her features. 'Let's agree to postpone the argument until after we've eaten.'

Lianne bit into a slice of peppered steak and almost sighed as it melted in her mouth. He fixed a mean steak, and the salad was crisp, the heated bread crunchy. She hadn't realised the extent of her hunger, or the pleasure in having a meal prepared and waiting for her at the end of a fraught day.

'Just as long as you understand it's definitely on the agenda.'

'I wouldn't expect any different.'

She caught the faint edge of amusement evident, shot him a dark look, and opted for silence.

'Perhaps you could enlighten me as to what Friday evening's legal affair involves?'

Lianne forked the last morsel of salad, replaced the cutlery on to her plate and looked at him carefully, noting the strength evident in his compelling features. 'I haven't been apprised of the details. This afternoon was the first I heard my presence would be required.'

'SMS me with a time.'

She finished her wine, declined a second glass, and began gathering china and flatware together, waving him aside as he rose from the table.

'You cook, I get to clean.'

'We'll do it together.'

There was a familiarity in their synchronicity that brought past incidents to mind when they'd chosen to eat at home and shared kitchen duty. Then they'd laughed, teased each other, shared a kiss or three and made love. Sometimes they reached the bedroom, occasionally not.

It had been wild, all heat and passion…and wonderfully evocative. She'd thought nothing could come between them.

Except Mette had been there, an intrusive, manipulative force with no integrity whatsoever…just self-motivated need.

Unresolved issues, Lianne reflected. Tyler's loyalty to Mette because of family connections. His avowal there was nothing between them except friendship. Lianne's doubt and confusion, making it difficult to separate truth from fabrication.

Now it wrought the question as to whether she should have stayed and toughed it out. Fought for the love of her life, her marriage...herself.

'All done,' Lianne announced lightly when Tyler had stacked china into the dishwasher and she'd dealt with the skillet and saucepan.

His close proximity unnerved her, and she held back the sudden need to lean in against him, have his arms close round her, and just be. Absorb his strength, confide the day, *share*.

For heaven's sake...what was the matter with her? Where was all the banked up anger when she needed it?

Tyler dispensed with the tea towel and turned towards her. 'Now might be a good time to clear the air.'

She possessed expressive features, and he wondered if she knew how easily he could read her. Or how badly she needed a diversion from whatever had caused the pensive introspection evident when she had walked in the door?

'The weekend thing?' Lianne pinpointed at once. 'Just what in hell were you thinking?'

'A preference for your personal opinion?'

She cast him a cynical look. 'Uh-huh. Like that's a valid reason.'

He leaned one hip against the servery and settled in

to enjoy their verbal exchange. 'You're a woman, you have knowledge of each location, and I can depend on your total honesty.'

'Flattery won't work.'

'No?' A slow smile curved his mouth. 'And I thought I was doing so well.'

'I don't trust you!'

'We've already spent a few nights together,' he qualified reasonably.

She opened her mouth, then closed it again. 'That's not the same.'

One eyebrow slanted. 'How so?'

Because it isn't sounded so…juvenile. 'It's not going to work.' She lifted a hand, then let it fall helplessly to her side.

His voice took on the quality of silk. 'Perhaps we should each accept the challenge to prove the other wrong.'

The air between them simmered with something Lianne didn't care to define. She was suddenly supremely conscious of every breath she took and the deep thudding pulse that seemed to reverberate through her body.

Her eyes locked with his. *'Why?'*

Tyler waited a few beats. 'You know the answer as well as I do,' he offered gently. He lifted a hand and cupped her cheek, let his thumb trace her lips, felt them tremble, then he lowered his head and touched his mouth fleetingly against her forehead.

'One down.' He lifted his head and his eyes held hers. 'You want to try for anything else?'

She wasn't capable of uttering a word for a few long seconds. 'It'll keep,' she managed, and saw his lips curve into a musing smile.

'I'm counting on it.'

CHAPTER SEVEN

THERE was a small degree of apprehension existent as Lianne rode the lift to Sloane, Everton, Shell and Associates' suite of offices.

She hadn't slept well. The prospect of that evening's legal soirée, Tyler, played on her mind. Top of the list was the weekend ahead.

Almost a fortnight ago her life had seemed relatively serene. She had gone to work, led a very low-profile social existence, kept in touch with family and friends.

Now it felt as if she'd been caught up in a whirlwind, tossed around and thrown way out of her depth.

OK, she would deal with it. A swift plea for celestial assistance might help with the day, the evening…why not try for the entire weekend? Surely she was due for a break!

The morning went by without a hitch. She elicited the time and venue for the evening, and SMSd the information through to Tyler, after which she completed a comprehensive check of the properties Tyler intended her to view on the Gold Coast and Port Douglas, then she marked in order her location preferences, subject to personal inspection.

It was after five when Lianne left the office. Traffic was heavy, providing a few snarls and delays which hampered her arrival home.

An hour was adequate time in which to shower, tend to her make-up, her hair and dress.

The door to the spare room was slightly ajar and she heard the shower running as she continued down to her bedroom.

Tyler. It gave her a jolt to admit she was becoming accustomed to his presence in the apartment, and she silently damned the swirling sensation making itself felt in her belly at the thought of his water-drenched naked body, the flex of muscle and sinew as he soaped and rinsed…and she tamped down the image of times past when she would have discarded her own clothes and joined him there.

Instead she took a solitary shower, washed her hair, then towelled dry. She used the hair-drier, tended to her make-up, then dressed with care, choosing a gown in jade silk chiffon with a delicately beaded bodice, spaghetti straps and a gently draped skirt.

Jewellery was confined to a diamond pendant, ear-studs and bracelet, and she slid her feet into elegant stilettos, caught up her evening purse and emerged from her room just as Tyler stepped into the hallway.

'Well-timed.' His eyes swept her slender frame with approval. 'Looking gorgeous as usual.'

Lianne returned the appraisal and inclined her head. 'You'll pass.'

'Thank you…I think.'

His soft laughter did strange things to her equilibrium, and she was about to make a snappy comment when her cellphone rang.

Except when she activated it, the connection was cut.

Tyler caught her faint frown. 'Problem?'

When she didn't answer, he caught hold of her chin between thumb and forefinger and forced her to meet his gaze. 'Don't hold back.'

'Why the third degree?'

'Is Michael Sloane's son bothering you?'

He didn't miss a trick. 'Why would you think that?'

A muscle tightened at the edge of his jaw. 'I've seen the way he looks at you.'

While I endured more than a *year* of Mette *looking* at you, she accorded silently.

Lianne held his gaze. 'Isn't that interesting.'

'Don't go there,' Tyler warned softly, and she offered him a singularly sweet smile.

'Wouldn't dream of it.' She waited a second. 'We should leave if we don't want to be late.'

Something shifted in the depth of those dark grey eyes, then he released her.

The venue was an exclusive inner city club where guests mingled and elegantly attired waiters served canapés and champagne.

Senior partners of noted repute vied with barristers and their peers who commanded a reverence second to none. Then there were the younger set intent on making a mark for themselves.

An eclectic mix, Lianne perceived, comprising the city's legal echelon. Add wives, girlfriends and lovers, and the full complement of guests had to number several hundred.

'Your inclusion is quite a coup,' Tyler noted quietly, and she summoned a polite smile.

'Due entirely to you.' At his raised eyebrow she

added, 'I was merely one of a dozen young lawyers until Michael senior lifted me out of obscurity and promoted me at your request. I could cry foul.'

'But you won't.'

'Lianne. Tyler.' Michael senior's greeting resembled that of a benign host. 'I hope you enjoy the evening.'

Appearances were everything, politeness essential, and Lianne acknowledged Michael senior and his wife, Michael junior and the stunning brunette at his side, whom Michael junior introduced as Janine, the daughter of an eminent judge.

'The favoured employee coupled with wonderboy...again,' Michael junior offered minutes later as he positioned himself at Lianne's side. 'Janine is weaving her spell as we speak,' he mocked quietly.

She summoned a winsome smile. 'Is that why you brought her along?'

'I needed a partner. Are you jealous?' His expression belied the lightness of his tone.

'No,' she said gently, aware she was treading on eggshells.

'Shame. We could be good together.'

It was fortunate that a fellow colleague joined them and the conversation took a less personal turn.

Tyler's introductory tour eventually concluded as he reached Lianne's side, and within minutes the guests were asked to take their seats in the banquet room.

Michael senior and his wife preceded their son and Janine, while Lianne followed with Tyler.

'Want to share?'

Lianne met his gaze squarely. 'Not particularly.'

'Independent,' he drawled. 'Stubborn, too.'

'It's part of my charm.'

'Uh-huh.'

'You're a babe magnet.'

His dark eyes gleamed with latent humour. 'Trading insults can be such fun.'

'Can't it, though?' she responded sweetly.

Their reserved table was already partly occupied with Shane Everton and Dante Shell and their wives.

Michael senior and his wife took their seats, and Janine very cleverly ensured she sat next to Tyler.

Great, Lianne thought cynically. A brunette bombshell bent on offering Tyler her all. Not to mention the need to project polite interest whilst conducting intelligent conversation with fellow guests.

Just what she needed to make the evening a *fun* occasion.

There were speeches, a few of which were staid and rather weighty, while another speaker utilised razor-sharp humour and had the guests responding with genuine laughter.

The food was superb, the wine representing some of Australia's best, and a slight 'roast' of one eminent legal eagle brought down the house.

Social events had been a constant during Lianne's brief marriage, for Tyler was known to support a few worthy charities. Women of all ages had been drawn to him, some overtly so, to the point where it had become almost embarrassing.

Yet he had rarely been far from her side, his light touch a given throughout the evening as he had sought to make it visibly known that while he might converse with women *she* was the only one who had any meaning in his life.

It had been evident in the light touch at the back of her waist, a hand tracing a pattern up and down her spine, the way his fingers threaded through her own.

She'd felt very much loved and secure.

Remembering made her heart ache.

'Let's escape, hmm?' Tyler intimated quietly, close to her ear.

Lianne offered him a faint smile. 'Janine will be disappointed.'

'I'm sure she'll cope.'

'Not without some reluctance,' she declared musingly.

'Whereas you are my concern.'

'Really?' Her smile widened and she batted her eyelashes for good measure. 'How…gallant.'

One eyebrow slanted. 'You want to continue playing the game?'

'Which game are we talking about?' she managed sweetly, and saw his eyes gleam with humour.

'Pick any one.'

'Oh, please. Spare me.'

Tyler leaned forward and caught Michael senior's attention. 'You'll excuse us? Lianne and I have an early morning flight.'

'Of course, Tyler. I'm grateful you could join us this evening.'

Lianne noticed the sudden hardening of Michael junior's expression, then it was gone.

'You're leaving?' Janine protested. 'I had hoped we might get a group together and go on to a nightclub.'

Her pout was pretty and obviously well-practised, Lianne accorded silently, sickened by the open invitation evident in those beautiful dark eyes.

Tyler merely smiled as he rose to his feet and inclined his head to their fellow guests. 'Goodnight.'

Lianne followed his lead and preceded him out to the lobby.

'Was that necessary?'

He cast her a direct look as he crossed to the bank of lifts and pressed the call button. 'What, precisely?'

'You know exactly *what*.'

The doors opened and they stepped into the lift, sending it to ground level.

'Setting a precedent?'

'Is that what you call it?'

The lift slid to a halt and Tyler instructed the concierge to summon a valet to deliver the Porsche.

'Aren't you forgetting something? You no longer have the right to dictate my life.'

His expression assumed a compelling mask. 'Give it up, Lianne.'

She compressed her lips and opted for silence, maintaining it during the drive home, in the lift to her apartment, and inside she made straight for her bedroom…only to be brought to a halt as Tyler's hands settled on her shoulders and turned her to face him.

Restrained anger emanated from his powerful frame, and she matched his dark look with one of her own.

Seconds, it had to be only seconds they stood in silence as anger faded and became replaced with something infinitely more dangerous.

Explosive, she registered dimly as it ignited between them and assumed a fiery passion.

There was nothing she could do…nothing she wanted to do to stop his mouth fastening on hers.

Hungry. She was so hungry for his touch, his taste, and she leant in, curved her arms round his neck, and hung on as he went deep, savouring the heat, the glorious sensual exploration of her mouth.

She wanted more, so much more. Skin on skin, and no restrictions. A bed. Dear God, she didn't care *where*…just as long as there was mutual possession and the slaking of an aching need.

There were small guttural sounds locked in her throat as she urged him on, almost begging as she pulled him close, and she was on the verge of tears as he gently withdrew, brushing her lips with his own.

For a few seconds he rested his forehead against hers, and she felt the supreme effort he made to regain control.

'Set your alarm. I want to be in the air by seven.' He carefully put some space between them and slid his hands to cup her face. 'Sweet dreams.'

His smile almost undid her, and she stood watching as he turned and walked to his room.

A single tear slid down her cheek as he closed the door behind him, and she moved blindly to her own room, too caught up with emotion to do more than lean against the closed door as she attempted to control the wild havoc raging through her body.

He'd been just as affected…she'd sensed it, *felt* it. Worse, he could have taken her and she wouldn't have stopped him.

So why hadn't he?

She closed her eyes in an involuntary effort to still the silent tears that welled and slowly rolled down each cheek.

No matter how she qualified leaving him or justified her actions, the desire they'd once shared was just as raw and primitive as it had ever been.

It seemed an age before she began to shed her clothes, and afterwards she lay staring at the darkened ceiling willing sleep and its blissful oblivion.

The sun was an opalescent glow in the early morning sky as Tyler's private jet lifted off the tarmac and rose to a cruising speed high above the northern Melbourne suburbs.

The colours were clear, washed clean by nightfall and a soft dawn dew, and there was no visible cloud to mar the landscape.

Within two hours they'd touch down at Coolangatta airport, where a hire car and driver would be at their service for the day.

Lianne had the property itinerary in her briefcase, compiled in location order, and inspections had been pre-arranged.

Efficiency was the key, she determined, and total dedication to the job at hand. Professionalism, and an absence of anything verging on the personal.

Sure. Who did she think she was kidding after a sleepless night filled with erotic images of nights past with the man seated opposite?

She'd woken to tossed sheets, discarded bedcovers and feeling an emotional wreck. Looked it too, and she'd felt only marginally better after a shower and her first shot of caffeine.

Smart casual wear was her choice for the day, and she'd selected tailored trousers, a crisp open-necked shirt and jacket and comfortable sling-back shoes.

The jet's interior was the ultimate in luxury and designed for comfort, with the pilot and hostess in Tyler's employ. It made for ease of travel, with provisions to conduct business, and there was a small bedroom complete with *en suite* bathroom.

Alysha, acting as hostess, showed no surprise at having Lianne on board, and her customary greeting displayed her usual warmth.

Coffee was served ten minutes after take-off, and was followed half an hour later by cereal, fruit and a cooked breakfast.

Tyler ate well, while Lianne picked at the cereal and settled for more coffee.

He bore the look of a man who'd slept well, and she banked down her irritation. It would have salved her indigence if he'd appeared as emotionally weary as she felt...not this vital male who emanated strength of will and an abundance of leashed energy.

Tyler had opted for black trousers, a white chambray shirt left open at the neck and a black soft-suede leather jacket which he'd discarded within minutes of boarding.

'More coffee?'

Lianne shook her head. Her nerves were already on edge. More caffeine would only accelerate her nervous tension.

Was she aware how fragile she looked? Tyler

mused as he observed her from beneath lowered lashes.

He wanted to scoop her up and hold her close. Except she'd probably fight against him, and he'd come too far to want to deal with any backward steps.

Patience was a fine thing. He was here for the long haul, not a quick fix. And he could wait.

Lianne withdrew papers from her briefcase and forced herself to concentrate as she ran a check of the data. Difficult when she was acutely aware of the man seated a short distance away. A whole day in his company seemed to stretch unbearably, and for the umpteenth time she cursed fate for being so unkind.

The *fasten seatbelts* sign clicked on sooner than she had expected, and their descent to Coolangatta airport was swift, the landing smooth, and in no time at all they cleared airport security and met with their driver.

Terranora Heights was first on the list, and the property was situated high on a rise on a large block of land with commanding views to the north, south and east. Not true country living, but the home was spacious and beautifully appointed.

From there they drove north to Hedges Avenue, Mermaid Beach, known to the locals as millionaires' row because of its beach frontage. Comprising three storeys and a basement garage, the home was perfection with nothing to fault.

Next was a penthouse apartment at Main Beach, with its private roof-top swimming pool and spa. Marble floors, exquisite features…as luxury apartments went, this was a dream.

'Lunch,' Tyler declared.

They selected a café at Tedder Avenue, chose a pavement table and ordered from the menu while the waitress delivered cool drinks.

Lianne extracted the list from her briefcase and prepared to provide an analysis, only to have Tyler close a hand over hers.

'We're on a break.'

Her eyes flared at his touch, and she was powerless to prevent the heat flooding her veins. Sensation unfurled deep inside and began spiralling through her body. It made her supremely conscious of every breath she took, and she was willing to swear her pulse was out of control.

Was he aware of the effect he had on her? Dear Lord, she hoped not.

She ordered a Caesar salad, and when it came she merely picked at it before pushing the bowl aside, her appetite gone.

The same couldn't be said for Tyler, who gave every appearance of enjoying his meal.

'Coffee?'

'No, thanks. I'll stick with iced water.'

He sank back in his chair and regarded her steadily. 'Michael Sloane junior. Tell me about him.'

She didn't pretend to misunderstand. 'He has a reputation for hitting on every new female employee under thirty.'

'Including you.'

She lifted her shoulders in a negligible shrug. 'Yes.' It had become almost a game...Michael junior asked and she refused. 'Just lighthearted stuff.'

'Which you handle.'

Lianne lifted her glass and took a long sip of cool water. 'Diplomatically. He's a golden boy, the head partner's son.'

Tyler inclined his head. 'I want your word you'll inform me if he becomes a nuisance.'

'Since when did you become my keeper?'

'From the day I first met you.'

His drawled statement curled round her nerve-ends and tugged a little. She looked away from him and pretended an interest in the street scene, their fellow diners and the beautiful people who lunched in order to be seen.

Minutes later she saw their driver return to the car.

'Shouldn't we be moving on?'

'Calling the shots, Lianne?'

'According to my schedule, we have a few more properties to view, including Tallai. I imagine you intend flying to Cairns tonight?'

Tyler pulled out his wallet and extracted a note to cover the bill, then he rose to his feet.

Sovereign Islands was next on the list, and the property he considered faced south, providing long sweeping views all the way down the coastal strip to Coolangatta. The interior design was something else, and delivered everything it purported to promise.

From there they took in Sanctuary Cove, Hope Island, and detoured inland into the hills to Tallai, where a veritable mansion sat high on a hill with acreage surrounding it and views in every direction.

It was almost six when the driver delivered them to the Sheraton Mirage where Tyler had made reservations for dinner.

The hotel was a splendid low-rise complex with a large tiled foyer and views over a cascading waterfall to the lagoon and ocean beyond.

The restaurant represented sophisticated chic, the food divine, and Lianne accepted a glass of white wine in the hope it would soothe her nerves.

All day she'd grown increasingly wary of what the night would bring, and whether her demand for separate rooms would eventuate. Worse, what she'd do about it if Tyler ignored her request.

'What time do you want to leave?'

Tyler didn't bother checking his watch. 'The pilot is on standby. I'll call him from the car.'

It was almost seven, and Cairns was about a three hour flight away. Port Douglas was an hour's drive further north, which meant...oh, hell, midnight before she could climb into a bed. Considering she couldn't recall sleeping at all last night ...

'You want me to do the Gold Coast property evaluation?'

Tyler ordered coffee, then leant back in his chair. 'We can do that during the flight north.'

If she could manage to stay awake. She'd been on edge all day, and it was beginning to get to her.

'Why not update me on your family? Your parents? Chris and Sharon?'

'They're fine.'

He offered her a quizzical look. 'Privileged information, Lianne?'

'Of course not. They have a two-month-old baby girl.'

'Whom I imagine you're looking forward to spending time with tomorrow.'

Her expression softened. 'Yes. Shantel is adorable.'

'We'll stay in Cairns overnight, and head out to Port Douglas early morning. We can be in the air again by nine.'

Tyler signalled the waiter for the bill, paid it, and rang for their driver.

Departure from Coolangatta airport was effected with ease, and Lianne extracted her notes once the jet reached cruising speed.

'It would help if you outline your preference.' She knew better than to factor in price. 'If you want capital growth and a high rental return—'

'I already have those figures. Which of the properties held more appeal to you?'

Lianne didn't hesitate. 'To live there on a permanent basis…Sovereign Islands. As a weekend and holiday residence…Hedges Avenue, Mermaid Beach.'

'Thank you.'

'That's it? You intend to close a purchase on my personal preference?'

'Yes.'

Oh, my. 'Why?'

'Because you have impeccable taste?'

He was teasing her, and she rolled her eyes, then replaced the report in her briefcase and gave him a steady look.

'Are you done?'

Not by a long shot, but he was getting there. 'Why don't you adjust the chair and relax.'

'Is that a polite way of telling me I look tired?'

'It's been a long day.'

The thought of chilling out and pretending to sleep for the remainder of the flight held definite appeal. 'Wake me when we land.'

He did, but not before he indulged himself with a last lingering look at her features in repose.

Beautiful fine textured skin, long natural lashes, a small pert nose and a deliciously curved mouth. Silky ash-blonde hair that smelled like fresh flowers…hair he loved to feel, slide his fingers through, or bury his lips in.

He longed to taste her, to trail his lips over every inch of her body, to tease, pleasure her until she sobbed, then screamed out his name as he buried himself in her moist heat, hold himself there, then begin a practised rhythm that would drive them both over the edge.

His loins tightened, *ached* with need. For her, only her.

He clenched his hands and thrust each one into a trouser pocket. Then he took a deep, calming breath and reached forward to lightly grasp her shoulders.

'Lianne. We're down.'

She heard his voice calling her name and opened her eyes, instantly alert. It was one of her useful traits. Even as a child she'd never burrowed her head into the pillow and wished the world would go away for another five, ten or thirty minutes.

Tyler held out a bottle of chilled water and she took it from him, drank long before re-capping it and rising to her feet.

Tyler had both overnight bags, and she caught up her briefcase and preceded him to the exit.

Within minutes of entering the terminal they'd secured their hire car and were heading towards a hotel in central Cairns.

Check-in at Reception presented a problem. The hotel was fully booked, and although they could confirm a two-bedroom suite had been booked, there had been a mix-up with Reservations and they'd been allocated a suite which had two double beds.

Profuse apologies didn't alter the situation. Yes, there were other hotels, but word had it all the major hotels were full due to a seasonal rodeo and circus in town combined with a major influx of overseas tourists.

The same suite, two beds. One night.

CHAPTER EIGHT

LIANNE looked at Tyler and could determine little from his expression.

'The alternative is Port Douglas.'

An hour's drive further north at close to midnight? I don't think so! 'The suite will be fine.' Her priorities were a shower, a long cool drink, and bed. In that order.

Within minutes they were on the correct floor and had located their suite.

Tyler deposited both overnight bags. 'Which bed, Lianne?'

'I get to choose?'

He sent her a quizzical look. 'You want to debate?'

He shrugged out of his jacket, toed off his shoes, then reached for the buttons on his shirt.

Time to make a decision! 'The one closest to the window.' She crossed to her overnight bag, extracted nightwear, toiletry bag, and headed for the bathroom.

It would be OK. Two separated adults, each sufficiently sensible to share a room without any awkwardness.

Who did she think she was fooling?

All day she'd been on tenterhooks, aware of everything about him, tantalised by his cologne, the way he smiled, his New York drawl. Being so close, yet so far apart.

It was killing her.

She soaped, rinsed, then towelled dry. She slipped on an oversized cotton T-shirt, brushed her teeth, drew in a deep breath, then opened the door.

Tyler was flipping through the pages of an in-house magazine, a towel hitched at his hips.

'All yours,' she announced lightly.

As soon as he entered the bathroom she slid into bed, switched off the bedside lamp and closed her eyes.

Lianne was aware of the moment he re-entered the room, saw him in her mind's eye slip between the covers, and heard the faint snap of his bedside lamp as the room was plunged into darkness.

Was he lying awake, as she was? Listening to the silence, as *aware* of her presence as she was of his?

Remembering the many nights they'd slept in each other's arms, wrapped together even in sleep after a long loving?

Did he crave her touch as she ached for him?

Oh, for heaven's sake, *get a grip*.

You're going to file for divorce. You want him out of your life.

So why in hell did it hurt so much?

She couldn't want him back, surely? Mette was gone, but what if some other woman took her place?

Go to sleep.

Agonising over what had been was a fruitless exercise. Predicting what the future might hold seemed equally ridiculous.

All she had to do was get through the night.

Except sleep continued to prove elusive as she

turned one way, then the other. She counted sheep, mentally reviewed the properties they'd inspected that day…correction, yesterday.

Nothing worked. She shouldn't have slept during the flight north. Although she doubted she could have stopped herself.

So, what was the solution?

If she'd been alone she'd have switched on the television and watched an in-house movie. Or flipped through one of several complimentary magazines.

A cup of tea would hit the spot…except she couldn't make it in the dark, and if she turned on the light it would disturb Tyler. And disturbing Tyler wasn't an option.

A drink? She could quietly filch something from the bar fridge.

The heavy curtains at the window ensured the room didn't receive a glimmer of natural night light, and she slid carefully from the bed, inched her way to the foot of it, then she calculated the distance to the console. Four steps, maybe five …

Her toe stubbed against something hard, and she put out a hand to steady herself, found no purchase, and tumbled on to the carpet. Worse, she hit her head against something on the way down.

'What the hell?'

Tyler's voice and the room flooding with light occurred simultaneously.

Lianne scrambled to her feet. 'I'm fine.' She put a hand to her head and felt a small bump on her scalp. Strictly *ouch* territory.

He was there, standing far too close as he traced the bump, saw her wince, then sought to check her vision.

'I'm OK.'

He hunkered down and checked her foot, lifting it for closer inspection, located the bruising, then he rose to his full height and took an icetray from the small freezer compartment.

'What are you doing?'

Tyler caught up a hand-towel, tipped ice-cubes on to it, made a cold pad, then applied it to her toe.

'If you dare tell me I should have turned on the light, I'll—'

'Hit me?'

He was amused, damn him! 'That, too,' she said fiercely, feeling impossibly angry with herself.

'Couldn't sleep?'

Lianne didn't answer. She was too caught up in the sight of him, his scent, the whole male package.

He was wearing black silk briefs, when he usually slept nude. An image of his tightly muscled body taunted her. So too did the memories...

Don't go there.

Except it was too late.

Oh, God. What was the matter with her?

'I'll make some hot tea.'

He moved to the servery, and that was worse. He had a great butt, broad back, muscular shoulders...and he was sending her crazy.

'I don't need a nurse.' Was that her voice? She sounded like a truculent child.

He didn't take any notice, and that irritated the hell out of her.

'Go get into bed.'

She threw him a dark look, met his measured gaze, and capitulated. Only to gasp out loud seconds later as he stacked pillows next to her own and settled back beside her. 'What do you think you're doing?'

'Your tea.' He handed over the cup and saucer and activated the television.

She didn't want him so close. Dammit, she didn't even want him in the same room! 'Go get in your own bed.'

'Afraid, Lianne?'

'Of you? No.'

'Good.' He folded his arms behind his head and gave every appearance of being engrossed in the programme.

Lianne gritted her teeth, then she sipped the tea and opted for silence. Minutes later she set the china down on to the bedside pedestal and pretended an interest in the show displayed on screen.

She had no recollection of falling asleep, but when she woke the room was still in darkness. Although there was a faint light behind the heavy curtains…dawn?

She moved cautiously, remembering…her toe felt a bit sore, but it didn't ache. Her head seemed OK. She stretched her legs, her arms, turned towards the centre of the bed…and encountered a warm male body.

Tyler?

He'd stayed in her bed? Slept beside her? *All night?*

She had to get out of here…

He moved, and she almost cried out, then the bedside lamp came on.

'Let's not run a repeat, hmm?'

His voice was a lazy drawl, and she didn't dare look at him.

'I've ordered breakfast for six.' He checked his watch. 'Should arrive soon.' He levered himself up into a sitting position in one fluid movement. 'You get first shot at the bathroom.' He leant towards her. 'But first, let's check that bump on your head.'

There was no evading his probing fingers. 'Hurt?'

It did, a little. But there was no way she was going to tell him so. 'I'll survive.' She slid out of bed, collected fresh underwear from her overnight bag, a fresh shirt, and crossed into the bathroom.

Tyler crossed his arms above his head, reflecting on the pre-dawn hours when Lianne had snuggled against him in sleep. He'd ached to pull her in close and bury his mouth in the sweet curve of her neck. To caress and kiss her into wakefulness and have her slide over him, possess him in a leisurely morning ride before he took command and returned the favour.

He never tired of her, nor she of him. She was a delight, so generous and giving…wicked. And the love of his life.

In one fluid movement he cast the covers aside and pulled on his clothes. He ran a wry hand over his jaw and collected his electric shaver and toiletries.

Lianne emerged minutes ahead of the waiter, and she let him in, directed him to lay the tray on the table, signed the chit, watched as he left, then she poured coffee. Hot, sweet, and black; it was just what she needed to kick-start the day.

Tyler joined her and they each did justice to eggs

Benedict, smoked salmon, toast and drank a refill of coffee. Then Tyler caught up their overnight bags, ran a last-minute check, and summoned the lift down to Reception.

Within minutes he'd fixed the bill and arranged for the hire car to be brought up.

The hills surrounding Cairns were dark with heavy foliage as they headed north. Cane fields lay fallow, and there were few vehicles on the road as their car swung towards the open sea. A scenic drive as the road hugged the base of the hills, following their many curves en route to Port Douglas, an isthmus comprising four miles from the main highway north.

Situated an hour's drive from Cairns, the Port was a thriving tourist mecca with numerous low-rise resorts, a magnificent golf resort, seafood restaurants, trendy boutiques, cafés, and four miles of white sandy beach.

Two properties were on the agenda. One an original cottage close to the township, the other a luxurious apartment in a fashionable complex.

Arrangements to view both had been pre-arranged, and Lianne completed the walk through, liked each, but the cottage won out.

'It's the beach,' she offered simply. 'The sea, sand, the feel of it. Relaxation, where sand on the floor doesn't matter. Some renovation and upgrading would pick it up a bit. Modernise the kitchen, bathroom, utilities. It has position, potential, the structure is solid…'

'OK. We're done.' Tyler pulled out his cellphone and rang the pilot. 'Let's go.'

They were in the air just after nine. Alysha served coffee, and Lianne made notes on her report, then sank back in her chair as Tyler worked on his laptop.

It was a companionable silence and she began to relax as they closed the distance between Cairns and Melbourne.

A seemingly fast trip, no stopovers, and they disembarked at Tullamarine airport to a brisk breeze and cooler temperatures.

They cleared security, collected Tyler's Porsche from the secure car park, and headed towards the city.

Lianne used her cellphone to ring Chris and tell him she'd be there in an hour.

'I take it Chris lives at the same address?'

Lianne spared him a quick glance. 'Yes. Why?'

'We'll go straight there.'

We? Her pulse went into overdrive. Have him drive up to Chris's home? Maybe have her family see him? The innumerable questions that would follow.

'If my parents see you—Chris—' Oh, heavens. 'It could be awkward.'

'I can do awkward.'

There was something in his tone that rang alarm bells. 'You're not thinking of joining us, surely?'

'You object?'

'Do you even need to ask?'

'Tough.'

'Tyler—'

He spared her a brief glance before returning his attention to the road. 'We attended a charity fundraiser last week, and a legal dinner Friday night.

Photographers were there, photos taken. Any one of which could be used by the media.'

And Tyler Benedict was newsworthy, she acknowledged wryly.

'Use your cellphone and alert them I'm with you.'

'You're not *with* me.'

'You want to argue? We're almost there.'

Lianne made the call, heard the surprised concern in her brother's voice, and knew *awkward* didn't cover it.

Act. Pin a smile in place and forget Tyler was there, she urged silently as he drew the Porsche to a halt in Chris's driveway.

Sure, and that's really going to happen, she dismissed. Tyler was one of the most unforgettable men on planet earth.

The front door opened and her parents were there, followed by Chris and Sharon, spilling down the footpath to greet her. Hugs, a comforting kiss, expressive concern…it was all there.

'Tyler.'

Barriers were existent beneath a façade of stiff politeness. A waiting, watching quality that spoke more volubly than words.

Family unity was strong. Tyler understood and applauded it, and would not have wanted less for her.

'Lily, Clive,' he greeted with a degree of polite reservation. 'Chris, Sharon.'

Sharon broke the ice by extending her hand. 'Tyler.' She indicated the entrance. 'Come through. Everything is ready out back. Shantel is asleep. But not for much longer.'

'Congratulations on the birth of your daughter,' Tyler offered. 'Lianne assures me she's beautiful.'

Sharon's smile widened and her voice acquired warmth.

'Thank you.'

It was a pleasantly warm day, and Lianne curved an arm round her mother's waist as they reached the back steps. 'Sharon has done wonders with the garden.' Already there were flowers in bloom, pinks, lilacs, a splendid array of gerberas.

'It's her passion,' Lily Marshall agreed as Clive and Chris began arguing peaceably as to who would cook.

Along with baking, sewing, various crafts, Lianne reflected fondly. Sharon was a born mother and homemaker.

'Chris is happy.'

Lily turned towards her daughter. 'Are you?'

Hidden meanings and unspoken words, yet the message was clear. 'It's…not easy,' she managed quietly.

'I don't want to see you hurt again.'

Didn't they say the first cut was the deepest? Walking away from Tyler had been the hardest thing she'd had to do. Picking up the broken pieces of her heart and patching them together ranked right up there. But she'd done it. Adding a protective shield had been a final touch.

Now Tyler was here, invading her space, her life…and each day it became a little harder to battle her emotions.

Did he know the inner turmoil his presence caused her?

Without doubt.

Clive turned as Tyler moved to stand at Lianne's side.

'What will you have to drink?'

Each man took measure of the other, something unspoken passed between them, and Tyler indicated the beer in his father-in-law's hand.

'That looks good to me.'

Marinated steak, crisp salads, crunchy bread eaten at an outdoor table beneath a huge shade umbrella made for a pleasant occasion.

Shantel proved her mother wrong by remaining quiet until they finished lunch. Then, just as Sharon rose to go and check, a startled cry sounded through the baby monitor and Sharon offered a light laugh.

'Perfect timing.' She turned towards Lianne. 'Want to come check out your niece?'

As if there was a need to ask!

Lianne followed her sister-in-law into the house and entered the nursery where an active baby protested volubly for a feed.

'Diaper change, hmm?' Sharon dealt with it efficiently, then she settled down in the rocking chair and put her nuzzling daughter to her breast.

Lianne felt an envious pull deep in her belly as she observed the special bond between mother and child. 'You make that look so effortlessly natural.'

'Now, yes,' Sharon agreed, then offered a faintly rueful smile. 'At first I thought we'd never be in sync with each other.'

'You never said.'

'You weren't exactly in the best shape at the time to share sisterly confidences.'

'Was it that obvious?'

'Only to those who care for you.' Sharon's gaze became startlingly direct. 'What's with you and Tyler?'

'Essentially he's here on business.'

'Uh-huh. You believe the business thing?'

'He has involved Sloane, Everton with the legal transactions.'

'Which you've been assigned to assist.'

'There's little correlation,' Lianne began, only to meet with her sister-in-law's expressive eye-roll as Sharon gently transferred Shantel to her other breast.

'Then why did he accompany you here today?'

If she revealed Tyler was ensconced in her apartment, Sharon would announce *game, set* and *match*. And it wasn't as simple as that.

'He's a masochist?'

Sharon shot her a quizzical look. 'You think?'

That was the trouble…she didn't know what to think. Just as she imagined she had a handle on the situation, Tyler changed the boundary posts.

'I think I should get to hold my niece,' Lianne said as Sharon lifted the babe and buttoned her dress.

'Prevarication?'

'Just…taking it one day at a time,' she responded as she reached for Shantel and cradled the babe against her shoulder.

'OK with me.'

Baby smells, a warm tiny body, the evidence of new life and love, Lianne mused as she encouraged a burp, following the obliging sound with a delighted laugh. 'Oh, good girl, darling.'

Sharon stood to her feet. 'We should go join the others. Lily has been itching for more baby time.'

The group of four appeared at ease as Lianne returned outdoors. The three men were engrossed in a seemingly friendly debate, while her mother busied herself serving coffee.

Almost as if Tyler sensed her presence he turned his head, locked his gaze with hers for a few heart-stopping seconds and let his mouth curve into a smile at the sight she made cradling Shantel.

Softened expressive features, her sapphire-blue eyes sparkling with deep affection, it was as if she had reached out and tugged at his heart.

He wanted the reality of the image she projected. The thought of a child, *their* child, brought him undone. It represented the whole package...the continuation of life. Theirs and that of their children. With this woman at his side. Only her. As it was meant to be...and had been for far too short a time before a manipulative, delusional woman had sought to tear them apart.

Had almost succeeded, he reflected, due to circumstances working against him.

Yet he was here now, and he would allow nothing, *nothing* and no one to stand in his way.

Clive Marshall glanced at the coffee swirling in his cup and felt a weight shift from his chest. He'd glimpsed a look in Tyler's eyes that a man didn't have the right to witness.

It might take a little while, but his girl was going to be OK. Stubborn, like her mother on occasion, he qualified. Tyler wouldn't have her fall easily into his arms. But she'd go willingly enough. And if Tyler had enough sense, he'd never let her out of them.

A slight smile caught the edges of his mouth. Unless he was mistaken, Lianne didn't have a chance.

It was after dark when Tyler eased the Porsche from Chris's driveway and headed towards Brighton.

'Hungry?'

Lianne spared him a sideways glance. 'Not particularly.' All she wanted to do was go home, take a shower, have an early night and catch up on some sleep. Tomorrow brought a return to work.

'We could stop off and pick up a pizza.'

'With lashings of mushrooms, onions and cheese?'

'Capsicum and pepperoni?'

'Done.' She knew just the pizzeria, and directed him to a small Italian family-run shop not far from her apartment.

It was great to kick off her shoes and ease the pressure on her bruised toe, shrug out of her jacket, and sit eating pizza out of a box at the kitchen servery.

Total relaxation after a hectic weekend, and she said so. 'This is the best.'

Tyler spared her a quizzical glance. 'Are we talking pizza?'

'That, too.'

It was good to see her eat after having her pick at her food all weekend. 'Another slice?'

Lianne shook her head. 'I'm done.' She slid off the chair and crossed to the sink, washed her hands, then she filled the coffee-maker.

She'd been supremely conscious of him all day. The way he'd leaned close when she pointed out something of interest, at the cottage, during the flight home. As for last night…let's not go there.

'I'll go unpack.'

A simple task which she completed within minutes, followed it with a shower, then dry. She pulled on sleep-wear and added a thick towelling robe before returning to the kitchen.

Tyler had discarded his jacket, undone a few shirt buttons and turned back the cuffs.

He'd dealt with the pizza box and two steaming mugs of coffee sat on the servery.

Lianne extracted painkillers from a high cupboard, filled a glass with water and swallowed the tablets down.

'Is that lump on your head bothering you?'

'I'm fine.'

Sure she was. He recognised the edge of pain evident in her eyes, the pale features. 'Why don't you go to bed?'

'I want to look over my notes.'

'They can wait until tomorrow.'

They could, easily. Except she wouldn't have time before she left for work, and she wanted to be able to hand Michael Sloane senior a report soon after her arrival at the office.

Lianne picked up her coffee. 'I'll take this in the study and drink it while I skim my notes.' She spared him a determined look. 'Fifteen minutes, tops.'

Tyler let her go. He needed to access his laptop, update his electronic diary and make a few calls. He also required to log on and check emails, which required accessing the cable connection in the study.

He checked his watch, decided to shower, made the requisite calls, then he checked the study and discovered Lianne still seated at the desk.

She glanced up as he entered the room, saw the laptop in his hand, and indicated the connection. 'I've almost finished.'

Tyler crossed to the desk and removed her reading glasses. 'You're done.'

His voice was a silky drawl and she looked at him carefully as she tamped down the swift rise of anger at his high-handedness.

'Give them back.'

He calmly collected her notes, put them in her briefcase, slid the reading glasses into their case and added them to her notes.

'You look like hell. Go to bed, before I put you there.'

'Bite me.'

'Try me much further and I just might oblige.'

'So who's a hero?'

'Five seconds to get out of that chair.'

Without thinking, she picked up her empty coffee mug and threw it at him.

Tyler caught it neatly and carefully placed it back on the desk, then he leaned forward and scooped her into his arms.

CHAPTER NINE

'PUT me down!' She bunched a fist and sank it against his shoulder as he strode out of the study and walked into her bedroom.

'Damn you.'

'So—bite me.'

She did. Literally, by sinking her teeth into solid muscle.

Tyler strangled a husky oath and slid her down on to her feet.

For interminably long seconds they glared at each other, anger uppermost, shielding something that went much deeper and infinitely more dangerous.

Lianne's breathing came thick and fast, and she could feel the pulse thudding at the base of her throat. The electricity between them was a potent, almost tangible force, and there was a stillness apparent in his stance, a waiting, watching quality she found vaguely frightening.

She stood mesmerised as his hands closed over her shoulders, then his head descended, angled in to hers as he took possession of her mouth in a kiss that punished as it demanded, seeking something from her she was reluctant to give.

Then the choice was taken from her as her body reacted of its own accord, driven by a primeval force as sensuality unfurled from deep inside, spiralling until

131

it totally consumed her, and hands that attempted to push him away slid up to link at his nape, holding him there as she edged the tip of her tongue to explore his, tentatively at first, then with a passionate fervour that blew them both away.

He slid one hand down her back and pulled her in against the heat of his arousal, then he fisted the other in the silky length of her hair and went in deep, caught the groan that rose up from her throat and eased back a little, softening the kiss until his lips brushed hers.

Her breath hitched as his mouth sought the sensitive cord beneath her ear and traced it down to the hollow at the edge of her neck.

Every nerve-end quivered at his touch, and she made no protest as he pushed the towelling robe from her shoulders.

Her own fingers were busy seeking hard flesh beneath the hem of his T-shirt. She heard his husky groan as she explored his rib-cage, and felt his body jerk a little as she teased each male nipple.

Then it was her turn to gasp as his hands slid beneath her nightshirt and cupped each burgeoning breast, then with an impatient gesture he dispensed with the nightshirt and pulled her high so she straddled him.

His eyes were dark, so incredibly dark she felt she might drown in their depths, and a choking sound escaped from her lips as he lowered his head to her breast and took its peak into his mouth.

Acute sensation arrowed from deep inside, radiating until it consumed her body, her mind…her soul.

With one fluid movement he drew off his T-shirt

and she shuddered as he dispensed with his briefs and positioned her against the length of his arousal.

Oh, God. She could hardly breathe as he urged her into a gentle rocking movement, and she arched back, giving him access as he began to suckle, taking her to the edge between pleasure and pain so she cried out, begging him to ease the ache deep inside.

He reached forward and threw the bedcovers aside, then he took her down on to the bed with him, gently rolling her on to her back as he trailed his mouth down to her navel, savoured there before tracing her belly, edging low until he reached the sweet heat bathing her highly sensitised clitoris.

All it took was one sweep of his tongue and she went up and over, almost crying out against the exquisite sensitivity he was able to evoke.

It became an emotive tactile invasion that sent her towards a explosive climax, and her fingers dug into the mattress as she held on, wanting more, so much more.

Now she wanted him inside her, plunging deep to ease the convulsing aching need. Except he seemed bent on tantalising her almost beyond endurance, and she beat his shoulders, begging him to desist.

Almost as if he knew she'd reached breaking point he rose up and claimed her mouth with his own, soothing with a gentleness that brought silent tears as her body shuddered with need.

It was then he entered her in one long thrust that wrought a silent gasp as silken muscles stretched to accommodate him.

She could feel the tenseness in that powerful body,

was aware of his control as he withdrew and plunged in deep, beginning a rhythm that consumed them both as he took her high, held her at the brink, then tipped her over in a shuddering climax.

Passion at its zenith, wild, all-consuming, *primitive*.

She didn't think she was capable of moving even the tiniest muscle as she cradled him close, absorbing the fast beat of his heart against her own, exultant in his strength as his heartbeat matched hers in a gradually slowing pace.

His mouth found hers in an open-mouthed kiss that was so incredibly gentle she found it hard not to cry, then he rolled on to his back, taking her with him, and cradled her close.

Gentle fingers traced the indentations of her spine, caressed the silken skin as she buried her face in the curve of his throat.

This, dear heaven…*this* was where she was meant to be.

She didn't want to think of the *why* of it. Just the here and now.

Slowly she began to drift as sensual exhaustion took its toll. As she slept Tyler carefully rolled on to his side and curved her in against him, holding her close through the night.

Lianne was lost in a hauntingly vivid dream where she lay wrapped in Tyler's arms, content, sated and in a pleasant state between sleep and wakefulness, not quite able to separate the dream from reality.

It seemed so real, for she could swear she felt the heat of his body curled round hers, the steady beat of his heart against her back and his warm breath stirring her hair.

She was almost afraid to move, unwilling to disturb the delicious sense of inertia. There was a lingering sensitivity deep inside, and she clung to it, loving the sensual ache of remembered intimacy.

A faint groan rose up in her throat. Any minute she'd wake and discover she was alone and the dream had merely been the result of her subconscious mind.

Then she froze as light fingers traced a path over one hip and spread over one thigh.

'Almost awake, hmm?' A deep drawl sounded close to her ear and she gave a startled yelp.

Tyler. Memory flooded back in an instant, the night, the argument...the loving.

She tried to move and failed miserably as he held her firmly while he reached out and switched on the bedside lamp.

Lianne was acutely aware of him, the look and feel of him, the warmth, the heat...and his potent arousal. His eyes were impossibly dark and slumbrous, his sensual mouth curved into a gentle smile.

Her eyes were wide, their depths explicit with a mix of consternation and disbelief. 'Let me go. Please,' she added with quiet desperation.

It was the *please* that did it, and he let his hands slide up over her shoulders to cup her face, then he angled his mouth over hers in a kiss that was so incredibly gentle it was all she could do not to cry.

Lianne scrambled from the bed as soon as he released her, and she fled into the *en suite* bathroom, turned the dial in the shower on full and stepped beneath the warm water.

Oh, dear heaven. How could she have let Tyler...?

A strangled sound emerged from her throat. She'd not only let him make love to her, she'd actively encouraged him. Had *begged*, she admitted in consternation. And had exulted in every moment.

She closed her eyes against the vivid image and groaned aloud in despair as she picked up the soap and began lathering her body.

Her breasts felt tender, their peaks still tingling from his touch. There were a few faint pink patches on her skin where he'd bestowed teasing love-nips, and the heat that still lingered deep inside from his possession.

Lianne became extra vigilant with the soap, lifting her face to let the water spray course over her body, only to give a startled yelp as the shower door slid open and Tyler stepped in to join her.

'What do you think you're doing?'

He spared her an amused look. 'Sharing your shower.'

He took the soap from her nerveless fingers and turned her round so he could wash her back. Then he caught hold of her shoulders and lowered his mouth to her nape and bestowed a lingering kiss to the sensitive pulse beating at the side of her throat.

'Don't.'

It was a defenceless plea he failed to heed as he trailed a hand over her belly, seeking the intimate heart of her in a wicked stroking that had her groaning out loud.

Lianne turned in his arms, linked her hands together

at his nape and held on as she angled her mouth to meet his in a kiss that tore the fragile tenure of her control.

In one single movement she rose up, wound her legs over his hips, and held on.

Tyler's breath hitched as she slowly slid up against his arousal, then down again.

'You want to play, hmm?' he queried thickly, and did some playing of his own, aware he was driving her as crazy as she drove him.

'Now.'

Her aching cry almost undid him, and he obliged, positioning her to accept his length as he thrust into the silken heat, then he shuddered as her inner muscles enclosed him.

Their coupling was wild and incredibly primitive, a passion that went right to the marrow of her bones and left her incandescent with a sensual joy so intense it was all she could do to bury her face into his throat and hold on.

For a while he simply cradled her close, letting the fingers of one hand trail gently down her back as he pressed light kisses into her hair.

He sought the sensitive curve of her nape and wrought a gentle massage, then he placed a hand beneath her chin, tilted it and brought his mouth down to hers, swept his tongue softly into the sweetness and lingered.

It was a while before Tyler closed the dial and, towelled dry, they emerged into the bedroom to dress.

Lianne caught sight of the time and saw she had

fifteen minutes in which to don clothes, fix her hair, apply make-up, gulp down coffee and leave.

'I'll go organise coffee.'

She spared Tyler a grateful glance as she pulled on fresh underwear, then she moved quickly to her wardrobe.

It was after eight when she entered the kitchen to discover cereal and fruit in a bowl and a cup of steaming coffee waiting for her.

'I haven't got time,' Lianne began as she reached for the coffee.

He'd tugged on fitted jeans and a black T-shirt that moulded every taut muscle on his powerful frame, and he looked, she decided, incredible.

'Five minutes.'

She ate standing at the servery, swallowed the coffee and caught up her laptop. 'Got to go.'

'You forgot something.'

Lianne looked askance at him in silence. 'What?'

'This,' Tyler drawled, and pulled her in. He lowered his head, bestowed a brief hard kiss and released her.

'I'll see you this afternoon.' At her puzzled frown he added, 'I have an appointment with Michael senior at three, remember?'

She raced out of the door, took the lift down to basement car park level, and battled traffic into the city.

Tyler. *Tyler*, a tiny voice echoed as she eased to a halt at yet another intersection.

What had she been *thinking*?

OK, let's pass on that one…she hadn't been thinking at all. Instead, her body had reacted of its own accord in recognition of an emotional force stronger than the dictates of her brain.

Where did that leave her *now*?

Sexually satisfied, a tiny imp prompted. Sure, and that was really such a help! Her body still tingled from his lovemaking…as it would for the rest of the day after several months of celibacy.

Had *he* remained celibate?

Another thought occurred simultaneously. He hadn't used protection.

Dear Lord in heaven.

The implications screamed through her brain. She'd stopped taking the contraceptive pill within days of leaving him. What if…? She did rapid calculations and almost breathed a sigh of relief. *Almost.*

Lianne spent the morning in a state of turmoil. Anger at her actions headed the list, with Tyler coming a close second.

She'd been a fool to let him stay in the apartment…not that he'd given her much choice.

If he thought they could slip back into a convenient sexual relationship…she wasn't going to let it happen.

Work intruded and she did her best to focus, cutting short her lunch-hour in order to keep pace with numerous phone calls and following up data.

Tyler's appointment drew close, and she was a mass of conflicting emotions by the time he walked into the office suite.

Cool professionalism, Lianne determined as she buzzed Michael senior and ushered Tyler into the huge book-lined office where the senior Sloane presided.

Tyler had, she determined, made up his mind and was determined to deal…on his terms.

Lianne didn't imagine they wouldn't be met. He had the wealth, business nous, and astute negotiating skills to make anything happen.

The meeting lasted less than half an hour, and she escorted Tyler from the mezzanine level to Reception, indulged in polite conversation, not a word of which she could recall within seconds of seeing him into the lift.

All she remembered was his musing smile as the lift doors closed.

Did he realise how confused she felt?

Without a doubt, she decided a trifle wryly.

What she needed was a diversion. No sooner did the thought occur than she picked up her cellphone and connected with Zoe via speed-dial.

'Coffee, darling? After work tonight?' Raucous music sounded in the background. 'For God's sake, turn that thing *down*.' There was a brief pause. 'Sorry about that. My assistant interprets *muted* as loud. Now where were we? Coffee. Can do. Usual place? Five-thirty?'

'Done.'

Lianne entered the trendy café a few minutes ahead of time, secured a table and ordered a latte. Zoe appeared just as the waitress delivered the coffee, added her order, then leant forward with an intent expression on her beautiful features.

'You did it.'

Lianne broke two tubes of sugar and stirred it in. 'Excuse me?'

'Slept with Tyler,' Zoe said without compunction.

'And you came to this conclusion…because?'

'Sweetie, you're an organised kind of girl. Spontaneous,' she qualified with an infectious grin. 'But organised. So when you phone me at four and suggest we get together at five thirty, I figure something's going on.' She paused for a few seconds. 'Tell me I'm wrong?'

Lianne rolled her eyes as the waitress presented Zoe's coffee.

'The question is what I'm going to do about it.'

Zoe broke two sugar tubes into her cup. 'Like you need me to spell it out?'

'It's not simple—'

'Sure it is. You love him. He loves you.' Her shoulders lifted in a shrugging gesture. 'What's the problem?'

'Unresolved issues.'

'So…resolve them.'

'Dammit, Zoe. I was going to file for divorce!'

Zoe leant back in her chair and assumed a thoughtful expression. 'Is that what you want?'

Life without Tyler? Lianne closed her eyes, then opened them again. 'I want what we had. What I *thought* we had,' she qualified.

'Which you'll have again, if you give it a chance and put what *was*, behind you.' Zoe was on a roll. 'Live in the present, not the past.'

'Easy to say, when the past intrudes on the present.'

'You're going to allow a vindictive woman to ruin not only your marriage, but your life?' Zoe queried gently.

Lianne retained a vivid memory of the cruel words

and heartless taunts Mette had issued. Those she had been able to handle. It had been the gossip leaked to the social pages she had found difficult to cope with. Given Tyler's public profile, the media had had a field day.

'I can't just slip back into the relationship and forget what happened.'

Zoe leaned across the table and covered Lianne's hand with her own. 'Your call, darling. But promise me you'll think long and hard before you make it. OK?'

Lianne finished her coffee and settled back in her chair. 'Let's talk about you. The new man in your life, work—'

Zoe lifted a quizzical eyebrow. 'Anything but Tyler?'

'Got it in one.'

'Joachim is Spanish, we've dated twice, he's adorable, and I think I'm going to have sex with him.' She gave a mischievous grin. 'You want more?'

Lianne broke into husky laughter. 'Definitely.'

It took a while, required a coffee refill before they were done, and it was after seven when they parted with a hug and the promise to get together again soon.

Tyler's black Porsche occupied its customary space next to her own as she parked beneath her apartment block, and she pressed a hand to her stomach to ease her nervous tension as she rode the lift.

It was crazy to feel like this, she decided crossly as she keyed in the code and opened the apartment door. What should she say…*Hi, honey, I'm home*?

She deposited her laptop and followed it with her bag. The shower wasn't running. Kitchen?

Lianne found him at the servery fixing a salad. Two steaks were ready to grill, and she could smell fresh bread rolls warming in the oven.

Her eyes skidded a little as she met his level gaze.

'Have you eaten?'

There was nothing in his voice she could fault and she shook her head. 'No.'

He'd exchanged the immaculate business suit for black dress jeans and a black shirt, unbuttoned at the neck, and he'd rolled back the cuffs. The total look was vaguely piratical.

There was an opened bottle of wine and two goblets on the servery and he caught up the bottle, poured wine in each goblet and handed her one.

'Tough day?'

Personally, yes. Professionally, not particularly.

'The usual.'

She looked tired. Strained, he qualified, and knew the reason why. It was the same reason she'd delayed returning home from work. He aimed to give her a few minutes.

'Want to talk about it?'

Her eyes dilated, and he glimpsed the nervous wariness apparent.

'Your day,' he elaborated, and saw her expression clear.

Lianne took a sip of wine, savoured it, then let it slide easily down her throat. 'Setting work in motion, paperwork, phone calls.' She effected a slight shrug.

'Michael senior is dedicated to providing you with one hundred per cent efficiency.'

Tyler leaned a hip against the servery and sampled his wine. 'I'm pleased to hear it.' His gaze locked with hers. 'Anything else?'

'We had unprotected sex.' The words came out in a rush, and she saw his eyes narrow fractionally.

'That's a problem?'

She was angry with herself, him…both of them for disregarding common sense. 'I haven't taken the contraceptive pill since…for months,' she added after a slight pause.

'There's a chance you could fall pregnant?'

'I don't know.' Did he have any comprehension how many times she'd done the maths in the past ten hours? 'I don't think so.'

'But it's close,' Tyler deduced gently.

'I can't be sure,' Lianne responded wretchedly, and steadied her nerves with another sip of wine. It was an excellent vintage, smooth on the tongue, slightly sweet, pleasant bouquet.

'Do you know how delighted I would be if you were to fall pregnant with our child?'

Oh, dear heaven. Six months ago she would have been of the same mind. But *now*?

Her hand shook a little. 'I'm going to file for divorce.'

'No,' Tyler refuted softly. 'You're not.'

She tried for stormy and failed miserably. Seconds later she gave a faint gasp as he took the goblet from her nerveless fingers and placed it together with his own on the servery.

Then he caught hold of her hand and pulled her in.

'What are you doing?'

'This.' His mouth closed over hers in a soft, seeking exploration that met with initial resistance, then she sank against him and held on as he went deep, taking what she'd been hesitant to give.

When he lifted his head she had little indication of anything other than the shimmering sensuality existent.

She didn't think she was capable of uttering a word, and a gentle smile curved his generous mouth.

'Go shower while I cook, hmm?' He traced a finger over her lower lip, then released her.

Lianne looked at him in dazed silence for a few seconds before turning away to do as he suggested.

The hot water spray had a soporific effect and, towelled dry, she donned jeans and a singlet top, then padded barefoot into the kitchen.

Food. The tantalising aroma proved a reminder that she'd eaten nothing since lunch, and she sat opposite Tyler, caught up her cutlery and proceeded to do justice to the succulent steak.

It was crazy to feel so…insecure, she reluctantly acknowledged. She was good at the art of conversation, so why couldn't she think of a rational thing to say?

'There's nothing you want to run by me?' Tyler queried with deceptive mildness.

Lianne cast him a careful look. 'As in?'

'Whatever's bothering you.'

'Why should you think something's bothering me?'

'Do you particularly want to play twenty questions?'

She replaced her cutlery and pushed her plate aside.

It irked that he read her too well. Worse, he inevitably seemed to be one step ahead of her.

'Last night—' She paused imperceptibly. 'Shouldn't have happened.'

One eyebrow rose. 'You consider it a mistake?' His voice was gentle, with an edge of something she didn't care to define.

It had been earth-shattering, and so *special* she hadn't been able to think straight all day.

'I don't want you sharing my bed.'

'Because…?'

'It's just sex.'

'Very good sex,' Tyler qualified solemnly.

Lianne could feel the anger deep inside take root and begin to grow. 'So let's continue where we left off, and forget the mischief and mayhem Mette caused?' Someone had taken hold of her tongue and was bent on letting it run on unchecked. 'You might conveniently be able to forget the scurrilous tabloid misconceptions drawn at the time. The inferences and implications, the ''no smoke without fire'' quotes. I had my every expression noted, examined, speculated upon, together with the constant media demand for comment on the—' she lifted each hand and formed quotation marks '—*situation*.'

Tyler regarded her steadily. 'I made a statement to the press at the time.'

'Yes.' She couldn't prevent the bitterness entering

her voice. "'I'm a happily married man, and I love my wife''.'

'You neglected to mention the... "There is no affair. My relationship with Mette is limited to a family friendship''.'

She'd asked the question at the height of their row. Now she asked it again. 'Did you sleep with her?'

'No.'

The image of Mette's sinuous body entangled with his acted like a stake through her heart. 'How do I know you're telling the truth?'

His eyes were incredibly dark. Anger? Remorse? She couldn't tell. 'You have my word,' he said quietly.

'The jury is still out on that one.' She'd reached this point numerous times during the past few months. Zoe's words of wisdom echoed inside her head and she closed her eyes in sheer frustration, only to open them again and stand.

In silence she collected the china and cutlery and transferred them to the servery. Then she rinsed and stacked them into the dishwasher, cleaned the grill and wiped down the sink.

When she turned, he was there. She hadn't heard him move, hadn't sensed it.

Tyler caught hold of her chin between thumb and forefinger and lifted it so she had to meet his gaze.

'I'd known Mette all my life,' he said quietly. 'We shared a friendship via family association. Our respective parents endeavoured to matchmake and while Mette got caught up in it, I never did.'

Lianne looked at him in silence. Trust, it was all a matter of trust.

The sudden peal of the phone sounded loud, and she moved away to answer it.

Her mother, stating she'd be in the city the next day and suggesting they meet for lunch.

Lianne did a mental preview of the day. In the morning she was due to view two residential properties with Tyler, and she wasn't due in the office until two.

She confirmed a time and place and assured she'd make the reservation. Maternal devotion was second to none. So, too, was Lily's desire for updated news. No need to guess on whom or why.

She replaced the receiver and stepped around Tyler. 'I'm going to have an early night.'

Tyler let her go. He had emails to compose and send, phone calls to make. A few hours, then he'd call it a night.

It was after eleven when he slid in beside her and gathered her close.

Lianne stirred, instinctively aware she was no longer alone, and she came sharply awake at the feel of his warm male skin, the steady beat of his heart against her cheek.

'I don't want you here.' It was a token protest, and she struggled a little as his lips brushed her forehead.

'Go back to sleep.'

'Tyler—'

'Shut up,' he bade gently. She curled one hand into a fist and batted it against his shoulder.

'You should go.'

He lifted a hand and trailed it down her back. 'Believe it won't be anywhere without you.'

She relaxed against him, too enervated to fight. 'You don't play fair.'

CHAPTER TEN

THE Mount Eliza property was first on the list…a large modern double-storey cream cement-rendered mansion, whose spacious interior was designer decorated and so impeccable it didn't look as if anyone lived there.

'No?' Tyler queried when they completed the inspection, and Lianne weighed her words carefully.

'It's magnificent.'

'But?'

'It has a sterile feel. Little character.'

The real estate agent looked vaguely shocked and began extolling all the advantages, only to have Tyler thank her and conclude the inspection.

Toorak was an older, well-established suburb with stately homes whose age and style set them apart from the more modern structures.

Leafy trees lined the streets, providing a gracious air, and Lianne almost held her breath as Tyler eased the Porsche between an open set of wide gates into a gently curving driveway.

The grounds were beautiful, lush green lawns, immaculate flower beds and topiary. But it was the house itself which drew her interest.

Established, aged, but impeccably kept, double-storey brick, a dark red tile roof, it seemed to reach out and touch her.

The agent led the inspection tour, and Lianne fell in love with the interior, the beautiful floor coverings, furnishings…it was perfection. As to the furniture…genuine mahogany antiques, exquisite artwork adorning the walls. It had character plus.

Tyler didn't need to ask what she thought. Her pleasure was clearly evident in her expressive features.

'Beautiful,' she accorded quietly, out of the agent's hearing. 'Everything. There isn't one detail I would change.'

'Good.' He thanked the agent, then led Lianne to the car.

It wasn't until they were heading in to the city he thought to relay, 'We've received an invitation to dine with Eleanora Postlewaite tomorrow evening.'

'Oh, my,' was all she could think to say, and incurred his enquiring glance. 'Eleanora is the equivalent of Melbourne's social royalty,' she managed drily.

'Showtime,' Tyler concluded, and heard her sigh.

'Definitely.'

It was almost midday when Tyler dropped her off adjacent to the restaurant where she was to have lunch with her mother.

Lianne entered the restaurant to find Lily already seated, menu displayed, and condensation beading tall glasses of iced water.

They greeted each other warmly, and a waiter appeared almost as soon as Lianne slid into the seat opposite.

'I know you only have an hour, darling. I'm going to order the Caesar salad.'

'Make it two.' She caught sight of a few brightly

emblazoned carrier bags at Lily's feet and she sent her mother a teasing look. 'Dad shouldn't let you loose in the city on your own.'

Lily gave a delighted chuckle. 'I've booked a facial and a manicure this afternoon. Tomorrow I plan to *do* Toorak.'

'Big spender, huh?'

'There's the most beautiful childrenswear shop on Toorak Road,' her mother said dreamily. 'I want to get Shantel something special.'

'You're spoiling her.'

'A grandmother's prerogative,' Lily assured her as the waiter presented their salads.

Any minute now her mother would mention Tyler. Sixty seconds and counting…

'Tyler's appearance must have come as a surprise.'

Twenty-five seconds had been all it took. 'You could say that,' Lianne responded lightly, and caught Lily's speculative look. 'Let's make this easy,' she offered with an impish grin as she held out one hand and began ticking off each consecutive finger. 'I don't know how long he'll be in Australia, or what his plans are. He's staying at my apartment, and, yes, we've had sex. I'm re-thinking the divorce.'

'Well, darling. That's interesting.'

'The sex was too much information?'

Lily offered a gleaming smile. 'I'm glad.'

'About what? The sex?'

Her soft laugh held a wicked tinge. 'Of course.'

'My unshockable *mama*,' Lianne mocked, and turned her attention to the salad. Wait for it…

'There's just one thing,' Lily ventured. 'All I want for you is to be happy.'

'Thank you,' she said gently.

They talked of other things, family, caught up on mutual friends, and all too soon it was time for Lianne to leave.

'Maybe we can do this again,' Lily opined wistfully. 'Soon?'

'It's a date.'

'I'll call you.'

Lianne spent a busy afternoon catching up with assigned files, and had almost completed the requested notations when Michael senior entered the office.

A long lunch?

'Lianne. My office in five minutes?'

More instructions, she assumed as she checked her watch and made a mental note of the time.

At precisely five minutes past four she knocked on the heavy panelled door and was bid, 'enter'.

'Come in, my dear, take a seat.'

My dear? She selected a padded leather chair and sank into it.

'I thought we should clear the air.'

Good grief, had she done something wrong? Was Michael Sloane senior about to prove office rumour correct and heap anger and reprehension on her hapless head?

'Tyler has chosen to impart certain information.' He sank back in his chair and regarded her carefully. 'You are, in fact, Lianne Benedict…Tyler's wife.'

Lianne felt the colour drain from her face. 'His estranged wife,' she corrected.

'He mentioned there had been a misunderstanding.'

She would kill him. 'An understatement. And it's personal.'

'Of course, my dear. I was not apprised of any details.'

She went straight to the point. 'Do you require my resignation?'

He looked vaguely shocked. 'No. Most definitely not.'

'Perhaps it might be best if my position as your legal assistant was given to someone else.'

'It does pose a conflict of interest. Tyler has indicated his Australian property portfolio is complete for the time being. However, I have other work I can assign to you.'

'Thank you.'

Michael senior rose to his feet. 'Splendid.' He crossed the room and opened the door.

She contained her anger...barely, as she returned to her office.

How long would it take for the news that she was Lianne *Benedict* to circulate? A day...two?

Right on top of that came the silent query...*did it matter*?

If anyone was sufficiently diligent they could access back copies of New York newspapers and photographic detail for themselves. It was all there...the marriage, high profile social events, reported gossip and, she imagined, their separation.

However the anger rode with her during the drive home, and by the time she entered the apartment she was shimmering with it.

Tyler was nowhere in plain sight, but she could hear the shower running. Within seconds she deposited her laptop, sent her bag after it, and strode down to the bedroom.

The door leading to the *en suite* bathroom was open, and she crossed to the shower stall, flung back the fitted glass door and launched into verbal attack.

'How *dare* you?'

His wet naked frame was a distraction she didn't need, and she tilted her chin and speared those devilishly dark eyes with her own. If looks could kill, he'd be dead.

'You're accusing me of something?'

Tyler's drawled amusement was the living end, and she reached on to the lintel for the plastic bottle of shampoo and threw it at him.

'As if you don't know!'

His expression didn't change, although his eyes dilated and became very dark. 'Come join me if you want to play.'

'Like hell.'

'Explain, or I won't give you a choice.'

Her chin tilted. 'Try it.'

He was way too swift. One second she was regarding him with belligerence the next she was hauled in beneath the pulsing water.

'Tyler! My shoes...my clothes—' She broke off and hit him, only to have him grasp both her hands in one of his as he proceeded to undress her.

'Stop it!'

Tyler paid no heed until every last vestige of clothing lay tossed in a sodden heap on the tiled floor.

'Now we're even.'

'That's a good suit!'

'It's replaceable.' His voice was a silky threat that did little to cool her fury.

'I hate you.'

Liar.

Heat swept through her veins, flaming each sensory nerve-end until her whole body felt as if it was on fire.

How could she be so angry one minute, yet so sensually alive the next? It was maddening, and at that moment she hated her own traitorous body almost as much as she hated him.

Tyler smoothed the hair back from her face and cupped her chin. 'Shall we start over?' His eyes held an indefinable quality she chose to ignore. He'd turned so the water flowed down his back, and she dragged her eyes away from the beads of water gathering on his chest and shot him a glittering look.

'You could have told me you intended to enlighten Michael senior about the marriage.'

'So you could delay it?'

Her lips tightened and her eyes became sapphire-blue shards. 'It'll be all over the office tomorrow.'

'And that's a problem…how?'

'I've led a quiet existence for the past few months. No hassles, no drama, no gossip to contend with.' It had been so peaceful without the media hounds baying at her heels, flash bulbs popping as they demanded a statement. She'd never felt so *naked*, so intensely vulnerable in her life. There was no way she wanted to tread that path again.

'Any gossip will be minimal.'

'Sure!' Her voice held infinite scorn. 'And cows fly over the moon.'

'I've issued a press statement announcing our reconciliation.'

Disbelief robbed her features of colour. 'You've done *what*?'

A muscle bunched at the edge of his jaw. 'It's done.'

'Retract it.'

'The media have done their homework.' Tyler watched the gamut of emotions in her expressive eyes. 'They intended printing an exposé in tomorrow's newspaper edition.' His gaze was steady, watchful. 'Damage control and a brief reconciliation announcement seemed a preferable option.'

Lianne had no difficulty imagining just how the original article would have run. It was all about selling copy, and the more sensational the spin, the more people would part with their cash to read the details.

'I see,' she said stiffly. 'Have you considered what my family will think? My friends? How do I explain a media-expedient reconciliation that isn't really a reconciliation?'

'We made love all through the night. What was that?' Tyler queried quietly. 'Just good sex?'

Maybe the first time, because they couldn't help themselves. But after that?

Lianne swallowed the sudden lump that rose in her throat. The sex had always been good. Better than good. A skilled lover, he knew how to please, and considered her pleasure before his own. So instinctively attuned, it was almost as if he was the other half of her.

'Slaking a mutual need.'

'You think so?'

Thinking was part of the problem. She'd done nothing but *think* since she escaped from New York. Convincing herself she'd made the right decision…the only decision that would ensure her emotional survival.

She'd been doing just fine until he had re-entered her life. Well, maybe not *fine*, but OK. From the moment she'd discovered him in her apartment, she'd descended into an emotional wreck. Aware, so damnably *aware* there could never be any other man for her, but *him*.

He was the very air she breathed. Everything she needed. All she could want.

'I want to spend the rest of my life with you, have children with you.' He shaped her face and held it. 'Grow old with you.'

The breath caught in her throat and her eyes clung to his as he lowered his head and took possession of her mouth.

His hands shifted, one to cup her nape while the other slid down her back and urged her close as he deepened the kiss into something so incredibly erotic she became lost.

It seemed an age before he lifted his head, and she could only stand there resting against him as she fought to regain a sense of reality.

Tyler held her and gently stroked her back, loving

the satiny feel of her skin, its softness, and the scent of her.

Then he lifted her chin and met her bewildered gaze. 'You want to lose this? Everything we are together?'

Emotion shuddered through her body. The answer was so incredibly simple…so right. 'No.'

He brushed his lips against her forehead, then trailed a path down to the edge of her mouth. 'Let's get out of here, hmm?'

'Five minutes,' Lianne murmured as she reached for the soap, only to have it taken from her hand as he gently lathered her skin.

Afterwards he snagged a towel and fastened it round his hips, before catching up another to pat the moisture from her skin. When he was done, she returned the favour, applied the hair-drier, then she followed him into the bedroom and pulled on clothes.

'Hungry?'

'For food…or you?'

'Both. It's just a matter of which comes first.'

Lianne pretended to consider. 'Food.'

'Order in, or eat out?'

It would be fun to add anticipation to the mix, to choose a small, intimate restaurant where the lighting was dim, the food divine, sample a little wine, feed each other, knowing that at the end of the evening they'd come home and make love.

'Out. I know just the place.'

Jeans, stiletto-heeled boots, a slim-fitting jacket, her hair swept into a loose knot at her nape, a touch of make-up, and she was ready.

Tyler matched her jeans, added a polo shirt and jacket.

'It's not far,' she assured as they rode the lift down to the basement car park. They took his Porsche, drove several blocks, and slid in to the kerb a few doors from a small French-style restaurant where they ordered superb wine, crusty bread and a magnificent veal dish with an assortment of artistically arranged vegetables.

There was a sense of *déjà vu* in the sharing of their meal, almost as if they'd gone back to the beginning of their relationship and were starting over.

Knowledge that hadn't existed before, a trial by fire from which they'd emerged intact. Wiser, perhaps, and more aware of human frailties. Less likely to take love for granted.

'Want to share?'

Lianne focused on Tyler's features and felt her heart turn over. For a few seconds she felt her eyes shimmer with the power of her emotions, then her lips curved into a winsome smile.

'Reflecting a little. How and where we met.' The magic, the electrifying sense of cataclysmic passion that had gone right through to her bones…the instinctive knowledge that this man was *the one*. The *only* one.

'No other woman came close.' He didn't touch her, he didn't have to. 'Not then, not since.'

She wanted so much to believe him. There was one question she had to ask. 'When will you return to New York?'

Tyler studied her expressive features and divined each one of them. 'Soon. With you. To visit family.

Something we'll do together a few times each year.'
He saved the one that would please her the most until
last. 'I intend Melbourne to be our home base.'

'You're serious?'

'Serious,' he assured. 'I'm negotiating office space.
Meantime, all I need is an internet connection, my
laptop and cellphone.'

'I think I love you,' Lianne said fervently, and heard
his teasing drawl in response.

'You mean you're not sure?'

She tilted her head to one side and pretended to
consider his query. 'Perhaps I should show you.'

She did it to him every time. The laughing smile,
the flash of white even teeth, the wicked gleam in her
vivid blue eyes.

'I imagine you want dessert?'

Her smile widened. 'And coffee.'

'Determined to make me wait, hmm?'

'It'll be worth it,' she promised.

It was, Tyler reflected several hours later. His groin
tightened in memory of her touch, the feminine witchery she employed to drive him wild. Beyond wild, he
added with a self-deprecatory twist of his mouth as he
recalled the primitive torment.

He had had his revenge, with a provocative tasting
that had turned exquisite torture into raw desire…and
passion which had shattered them both.

'Hmm, your heartbeat just picked up,' Lianne said
huskily. 'Lustful thoughts?'

Tyler let his fingers continue their drifting up and
down her spine. 'You'll be the death of me.'

She let her hand slide down to his arousal and

gently stroked it. 'Not for a hundred years.' Her fingers trailed up and settled on his shoulder, then she closed her mouth over one male nipple. 'You want to take a bubble bath?'

'Minx. Sleep first.'

CHAPTER ELEVEN

THE reconciliation item appeared on the social page of the morning newspaper, together with a small photograph taken at the Charity Benefit and filched from the media files.

With luck it would pass unnoticed by most, Lianne determined as she entered the exalted offices of Sloane, Everton, Shell and Associates.

She greeted the girls manning Reception and went directly to her office on the mezzanine level.

It was work as usual, although not on Tyler's property portfolio. A file sat on her desk with detailed instructions from Michael senior, and she perused it carefully, making notations as she went.

Mid-morning there was a conference call with Michael senior and the client, and she had barely returned to her desk when her phone rang.

'Aren't you the secretive one?' Michael junior's voice held cynical amusement.

She'd play it cool. 'Michael,' she acknowledged. 'I'm busy right now. Can I get back to you?'

'I wanted to offer my congratulations.'

'Thank you.'

'Never stood a chance, did I?'

Honesty and tact didn't always go together, but she tried. 'I chose not to date anyone.'

'I imagine you'll resign.'

'I have another call waiting.' She didn't, but it enabled her to cut the connection.

Minutes later her cellphone beeped with an incoming text message. Zoe. Suggesting lunch at the usual café at one. It took only seconds to key in an affirmative reply.

The world, *her* particular world, seemed a brighter place. The sun shone, and there were no hovering clouds to dull the day, either literally or figuratively.

Zoe was already seated and there were two cups of steaming coffee reposing on the table.

'I ordered so we won't be interrupted,' Zoe declared as Lianne slid into the chair opposite. '*Give*, girl,' she commanded with a wicked grin. 'What's with the reconciliation announcement?'

'It's partly damage control.'

Zoe's eyes narrowed. 'A media diversion?'

'In a way.'

'OK. So where does this leave you?'

'I'm…working on it.'

'Sounds promising.'

'Maybe.' It was too new for her to want to talk about it with anyone just yet.

Zoe gave a dejected sigh. 'Not going to tell me, are you?'

A waitress delivered their salads, and Lianne picked up her fork, toyed with the various greens, then she speared a segment of smoked salmon.

Lianne opted for partial truth as she met Zoe's intent gaze. 'My aim in leaving New York was to heal and move on with my life.'

'Now Tyler is messing with those plans.'

Wasn't that the truth!

'Meanwhile, you're enjoying the sex.'

It was more than that, except she wasn't ready to admit it to anyone just yet. 'Is that so bad?'

'Sweetheart,' Zoe derided gently, rolling her eyes. 'Give me a break!'

An insistent burr sounded and Zoe retrieved her cellphone. The call was brief and her expression held regret as she cut the connection. 'I'm going to have to leave in a few minutes.'

'That's OK. Eat,' Lianne bade. 'Lunch is on me.'

'That's not how it works.' Within seconds Zoe placed a note on the table and it was Lianne's turn to roll her eyes.

'Stubborn.'

Zoe finished the last of her salad, drained her coffee, then offered an irrepressible grin. 'Right back at you.'

'How are things progressing with Joachim?'

Zoe's expression sobered a little. 'A little edgy.'

'I'm sorry.' Her concern was genuine.

Zoe checked her watch. 'Gotta go.' She stood, did the air-kiss thing, and lightly touched Lianne's shoulder. 'Take care.'

'Always. You, too.'

Lianne managed to leave the office at five that evening, dealt with peak hour traffic exiting the city, and she entered the apartment with little more than three-quarters of an hour in which to shower and dress.

The thought of attending a dinner party didn't hold much appeal. Yet Tyler had accepted the invitation and she could hardly opt out, given the media announcement of their reconciliation.

She was about to step out of the shower when she heard the front door close, and within minutes Tyler entered the *en suite* bathroom.

Lianne sent him a dark glance. 'There *is* another bathroom.'

His voice was an amused drawl. 'I had hoped to share yours.'

'Too late,' she said succinctly as she wrapped a towel round her slender curves and tucked the edge between her breasts.

'You could always join me.'

'No,' she retorted. 'I couldn't.'

The next instant she gave a startled yelp as he pulled her close and fastened his mouth over hers in a provocative kiss that almost persuaded her to change her mind.

'What was that for?'

He framed her face and traced the outline of her mouth with one thumb. 'To give you something to think about during the next few hours.'

Her expression was priceless, and without a further word he stepped into the shower stall, closed the door, and turned on the water.

Lianne selected a black classic-style dress, added a beaded jacket, stilettos, and swept her hair into a smooth chignon. Make-up received careful attention and she slipped on minimum jewellery.

Tyler stood waiting for her in the lounge, and her heart lurched at the sight of him. The impeccably-cut black dinner suit accentuated his height and breadth of shoulder, and she had no need to imagine the body beneath the fine tailoring. She knew it too well, the shape and feel of it, the hard ridge of muscle and sinew, the warm flesh.

Oh, get a grip, she chastised silently as they rode the lift down to the basement car park.

Tyler eased the Porsche on to street level and spared her a brief glance. 'You'll need to direct me.'

Eleanora Postlewaite, of the socially elite Postlewaites, resided in a mansion befitting her status in the old monied suburb of Toorak, and Lianne felt an onset of nervous tension as Tyler cut the engine.

'Ready?'

She met his query with a graphic eye-roll. 'To face the fray?'

'Leave it to me to answer any questions.'

'And that's going to work? The social requirement for successful gossip-gathering is to divide and conquer,' she alluded with wry cynicism.

'Not if we appear joined at the hip.'

'Ah, I'll adopt the adoration strategy. Soft and dreamy and oblivious to everyone but you?'

'It's only a few hours.'

'There are occasions when *a few hours* seem a lifetime.'

And this was definitely going to be one of them, Lianne determined as they were greeted at the door by no less than Eleanora herself, and welcomed with the enthusiasm usually reserved for very dear close friends.

Tyler's reputation preceded him, Lianne granted silently as she accepted their hostess's air-kiss.

One minute…two?

'How lovely to read of your reconciliation.'

Lianne was out by one. Eleanora had waited three minutes before launching into the social news of the moment.

'Thank you.' Tyler's New York drawl, combined with his displayed charm and generous smile was enough to make any woman's pulse-rate soar.

'I'm delighted for you both.'

Of course, Lianne conceded. It has provided you with a social coup no other social doyenne can match. Pamela Whitcroft will be green with envy.

'Come through to the lounge where the guests are assembled, and I'll perform the introductions.'

Oh, my. The guests represented some of Melbourne's *names* Lianne was familiar with… captains of industry with their partners, a tireless charity organiser of high repute, a fashionista. Recognisable, vaguely intimidating, and eager for the latest in news.

Carefully concealed, of course, beneath polite warmth and seeming friendship.

Lianne's year as Tyler's wife in New York had served as a learning curve, for she knew how to play the social game and play it well. Consequently she assumed an expected persona, accepted a glass of fine wine and, thanks to Tyler's apparent devotion, remained firmly at his side…despite a few subtle attempts to separate them.

Dinner was served at eight, in a magnificent formal dining room where a large table was set for twenty-four guests.

Immaculate damask, crystal, silver flatware, exquisite bone china, floral decorations…the setting was a work of art. So too were the name-cards nominating the seating arrangement.

Two uniformed waitresses were on hand to serve, and a wine steward ensured there was no lapse in the replenishing of liquid refreshments.

Conversation was varied and faultless, the various courses attributed to an excellent chef, and throughout the seemingly endless meal Lianne was aware of Tyler's every move.

The light touch of his hand on her arm, the warmth of his smile. The latent sensuality in those dark eyes had the most disturbing effect on her equilibrium, and it hurt unbearably to know he was only acting a part.

The thought of his lovemaking, the passion they'd shared, confounded her on one level and confused her on another.

She'd been *with* him, part of him, all the way. So caught up in their shared sexual energy she had had no thought for anything else, only the *now*.

How could she feel like that when she was still in a state of ambivalence?

'Lianne,' Eleanora cajoled with polite warmth. 'Do tell us the story behind your recent reconciliation.'

There was a telling silence from their fellow guests, almost as if everyone was tuning in to about-to-be revealed momentous news.

What took you so long? she wanted to ask, only to give herself a mental slap on the wrist.

Lianne cast Tyler a sparkling glance. 'Shall I, darling? Or will you?' Pass the ball, *please*.

He caught hold of her hand and lifted it to his lips. His gleaming gaze was for her alone. 'You, darling.'

'It's quite simple,' she revealed with just the right degree of musing reflection. 'I took time out.'

'Really? One can only wonder why.'

A logical assumption to those with different values and morals, when wealth was *God*, and wives turned a blind eye to a husband's philandering.

However, the words never left her lips. Instead she gave Eleanora a winsome smile. 'Perhaps I wanted him to choose.'

She could almost sense the sound of a pin dropping in the resulting silence.

'Naturally, there could only be one choice,' Tyler accorded with indolent ease as he caught Lianne's hand and lifted it to his lips. 'Lianne.'

'So romantic,' Eleanora rhapsodised to murmurs of assent from fellow guests.

Lianne added gloss to the gilt by casting Tyler a misty smile. 'I think so.'

Eleanora, ever the gracious hostess, suggested, 'Shall we adjourn to the lounge for coffee and liqueurs?'

It was eleven before they were able to leave, amid verbal invitations to future events for which written confirmation would follow.

'Nothing to say?' Tyler voiced as he sent the Porsche into the night streets.

Lianne met Tyler's musing gaze. 'Try all talked out from playing the role of devoted wife,' she returned solemnly, and heard his husky chuckle.

'It will have broken the ice.'

'The temptation to shatter it was strong.'

'Should I offer thanks for your reticence?'

'Definitely.'

He directed a teasing glance. 'I'm sure I'll think of a suitable reward.'

'For good behaviour?'

'That, too.'

He did, very thoroughly. As a reward it beat anything tangible, hands down.

Emotional euphoria at its zenith, Lianne accorded, sensually replete as she drifted off to sleep in Tyler's arms.

The next day began well with a leisurely breakfast, after which Tyler left for the airport *en route* to a meeting in Sydney, while Lianne headed into the city in her Mini Cooper.

Michael senior called her into his office to confer over a client's conveyancing issue and discussed the day's agenda.

Lunch was something she sent out for and ate at her desk while she perused text in a book borrowed from the firm's law library.

It was after four when Michael senior asked her to sit in on a client consultation. At the appointment's conclusion the client brought up his interest in aviation, expounded on privately owned aircraft in particular and the pilots employed to fly them.

'A Lear jet owned by some American tycoon went down about an hour ago. Explosion on emergency landing. Heard it on the car radio as I drove into the city.'

For one horrible moment Lianne went completely blank and felt the colour drain from her face. 'Was it on a flight plan from Sydney?'

'I believe so.'

'Tyler?' Michael senior queried of Lianne at once, and used the inter-office intercom to summon his personal assistant to show the client to the lift.

Lianne indicated the desk telephone. 'May I?'

'Of course.'

She keyed in Tyler's cellphone number and waited with bated breath for it to connect, only to hear the out-of-range tone.

Fear clutched hold of her heart and squeezed tight, almost robbing the breath from her body. Come on, *come on*, she begged silently, and pressed *redial*, only to get the same result.

Michael senior crossed to the desk, caught up his cellphone and handed it to her. 'Keep trying, while I make some enquiries.'

'It may not be Tyler. We should be able to access the relevant details.'

It became a nightmare as various phone calls merely confirmed that details could not be officially released until the aircraft had been positively identified, together with the pilot and passenger.

Repetitive calls to Tyler's cellphone resulted in a constant out-of-range tone, and Michael senior insisted she drink the tea he had his secretary bring as he endeavoured to use his influence to determine facts.

Lianne began bargaining with the Deity, painfully aware that there was no price she wouldn't pay for Tyler's survival.

Nothing else held any significance in her life, and she knew she would cease to exist if Tyler wasn't there to share it with her.

She began to shake, and tried to control it. Then she went into a state of icy calm.

It seemed to take for ever before Michael senior cut the last call and turned to face her.

'It's not Tyler.'

Lianne almost collapsed with relief, and drew a shuddering sigh as she attempted to control her emotions.

'You're sure?'

'Positive.' He relayed facts in reassurance. 'His aircraft is confirmed as just having landed. Give me the cellphone, and I'll call him.'

He pressed *redial* and within seconds Lianne heard him providing a concise report. Then he handed the cellphone to her.

'Lianne?'

The sound of Tyler's familiar drawl tore the breath from her throat.

When she could speak she said the words which held precedence over anything else. 'I love you.'

Sweet merciful mother of God. Tyler's fingers gripped the cellphone. 'Stay where you are until I get there,' he said gently. 'I'm on my way.'

She closed her eyes and summoned a degree of inner strength. 'I'm fine.'

The hell she was. Tyler slid behind the wheel of his Porsche and sent it growling out of the terminal car park.

'Would you like more tea, my dear?'

Lianne shook her head and stood to her feet. 'Thank

you for your help.' She felt like a robot, operating by remote control. 'I'll go back to my office.'

Michael senior looked at her with concern. 'I'll instruct my secretary to sit with you until Tyler arrives.'

'I'll be fine. Really.'

'I must insist.' Tyler's instructions had been specific.

Lianne had little recollection of exactly what transpired after that. She remembered walking to her office and sitting at her desk. There was more hot sweet tea put in front of her, which she sipped absently while Michael senior's secretary occupied her with conversation regarding subjects she later failed to recall.

Then Tyler was there, looming large in a room that suddenly seemed too small.

Lianne half-rose from the chair as he inclined his head in acknowledgement of the secretary's presence. 'Please close the door on your way out.'

It said much that the woman didn't even question him as she left the room.

Lianne.

If he lived to be a hundred, he would never forget the expression in those beautiful sapphire-blue eyes as they held his.

Naked emotion laid bare. For him, only him.

He reached her in seconds and pulled her in against him. Then, without a word, he fastened his mouth on hers, gently at first, parting her lips with his own as he savoured the sweetness.

He needed to alleviate her fear, dispense the anxiety, and replace both with reassuring proof.

Afterwards would come the words.

His tongue took a sensuous glide over hers, teasing a little as he held her hair with one hand while the other cupped her bottom and held her close against him.

Lianne wound her arms around his neck and held on, loving the feel of him, his warmth, the evidence of life in his beating heart.

She angled her head and held his mouth captive as she deepened the kiss with hungry passion. And love.

It was apparent in her touch, the stifled throaty moans of desire and the sensual heat of her body.

With exquisite slowness Tyler began easing back, then he lifted his head and pressed his forehead against her own.

'Let's go home.'

He threaded his fingers through her own and led her to the door.

'My bag…keys. My car,' Lianne protested, and met the passion evident in his dark gaze.

'You won't need them.'

They rode the lift, walked to where Tyler had parked the car and joined the peak hour traffic vacating the city.

'I thought I'd lost you.' Was that her voice? It sounded different…almost breathy, soft. Dammit, *forlorn*.

Without a word he caught hold of her hand and pressed it against his cheek, held it there until he needed to relinquish it to change gear.

No sooner had the apartment door closed behind them than Tyler swept her into his arms.

'What are you doing?'

He pressed a brief hard kiss to her mouth. 'Taking you to bed.' The one place where he could prove beyond doubt he was very much alive.

A faint smile curved her lips. 'You are?'

'Uh-huh.' He reached the bedroom, let her slide to her feet, shucked off his jacket, removed his tie, and began divesting her of clothes.

He got as far as her bra and briefs when she caught hold of his hands, stilling his actions.

'Please,' she began quietly. 'There's something I need to say first.'

The warmth of his smile almost undid her.

'The past few hours were the worst in my life.' There was more. 'The thought of losing you…' Her body trembled of its own accord. 'You're my life.' She lifted a hand and laid it against his cheek. 'Everything I could ever want or need,' she vowed gently. 'Always.'

His mouth angled close to hers and she lightly traced his lips. 'I'm not quite done.'

'No?'

'I love you.' The words were achingly heartfelt. 'So much.'

Tyler closed his eyes, then opened them again, and Lianne almost died at the depth of emotion in those dark depths.

'You have my heart,' he vowed softly. 'My love. Always.'

He took her mouth with his own in a sensual exploration that fanned the heat, the passion, and she was hardly aware of moving until she felt the mattress beneath her back.

What followed was an oral feast of the senses, and a possession which shattered them both with its intensity.

Lovemaking. The merging of two souls in perfect accord, Lianne decided dreamily as they lay together in each other's arms.

She didn't feel inclined to move. Doubted she even could.

Eventually, in the depths of night, hunger drove them into the kitchen. Together they fixed omelettes, toast, fed each other morsels, then retreated to bed to sleep... Only to wake in the early dawn hours and indulge in a leisurely loving.

Life...hers, Lianne qualified as Tyler drove her into the city, was wonderful. Magical, she added for good measure as she planted a swift kiss on his cheek seconds after he pulled in to the kerb immediately adjacent to her office building.

'Take care,' she bade softly, then gasped as his mouth fastened on hers in a brief, hard kiss.

'Always.' His voice held teasing assurance as he watched her slip out from the Porsche.

Work took on a hectic pace as the day progressed, exacerbated by the need to make personal courtesy phone calls to several members of Michael senior's client base, informing them of the name of the firm's lawyer filling in during her month's leave of absence.

Lianne's cellphone rang just as she was about to leave the office. She took the call and discovered Chris on the line.

'You haven't forgotten the farewell family get-together tomorrow afternoon?'

'Three, at your place,' she reiterated. 'I'll bring dessert.'

'Sharon's got it covered,' Chris assured her.

At that moment the lift doors opened and she cut the connection.

Lianne collected seafood at her local supermarket, added various salad greens, caught up a baguette and took them through the check-out.

The car space beside her own beneath the apartment building was empty, which meant she had time to shower and change before Tyler arrived home.

She'd just put the finishing touches to the meal when he walked in the door.

'Hmm, something smells good.' His jacket was hooked over one shoulder and he had already loosened his tie as he crossed to where she stood and covered her mouth with his own. 'Give me five minutes to shower and change.'

They took their time with the meal, exchanging news of the day, shared anecdotes. Then, kitchen duties complete, they settled comfortably together and watched a movie on the DVD player.

'Early night, I think.' Tyler scooped her into his arms and carried her through to the bedroom, where they slept curled together until morning.

CHAPTER TWELVE

IT WAS a beautiful day, with an azure sky, very little cloud, and the sun's warmth fingered the earth. The lawns were a lush green and almost every suburban garden bore colourful flowers in bloom.

Lianne sat back, relaxed and content as Tyler eased the Porsche on to the Nepean Highway and headed towards the city.

So much had happened in so short a time, she reflected, for within a matter of weeks Tyler had swept back into her life, taken control, and effected the impossible.

It was a measure of the man, his strength, power and determination.

He'd made her aware that their love for each other went so deep that nothing and no one could touch it.

Tomorrow her parents were due to drive back to Geelong, and in a week's time she would fly with Tyler to New York.

A request for a month's leave of absence from Sloane, Everton, Shell and Associates had been granted without question...doubtlessly a conciliatory gesture to her recognised status as Tyler Benedict's wife.

'Pleasant thoughts, I hope?'

Tyler's drawling voice intruded and she gave him a stunning smile. 'How could they not be?' The vivid

178

memory of last night's loving stayed with her, and she felt the customary ache deep within as she met his gleaming gaze.

The traffic lights changed and he returned his attention to the road, swinging into a lane which only permitted a right turn.

'You probably should have gone straight ahead.' She indicated the intersection a short distance away. 'You'll be able to turn left there.'

Except Tyler veered to the right and incurred her puzzled look. 'There's been a slight change in plan.'

'We're not going to Chris and Sharon's place?'

He changed gears and made it through the intersection on an amber light. 'Not today.'

'We *are* meeting with them and my parents?'

'Of course.'

She sent him a teasing glance. 'If I ask, are you going to tell me?'

'Tell you what?' His voice held amusement and she shook her head at him.

'OK, I give up.' A picnic in the park? Or maybe a restaurant? Whatever, it hardly mattered.

Toorak? She silently questioned as he entered High Street. She would have thought Southbank...

It wasn't until he turned into a familiar street and bypassed another that suspicion teased her mind.

He hadn't... No, he couldn't possibly have... If he made a left turn into the next street....

When he did, she gave him a faintly shocked look, which he ignored as he eased speed in order to swing in to a gated entrance.

The same gated entrance leading to the Toorak

property she'd expressed delight in when they'd viewed it together.

At the touch of a small remote device the gates swung open, and Tyler took the curved driveway to the front portico.

'Welcome to our new home,' Tyler said as the Porsche slid to a halt.

'You *bought* the house?' She could hardly believe it. 'Tyler…' It wasn't often she was speechless. 'It's beautiful,' she managed at last. In a spontaneous gesture she captured his face, leant in and kissed him, then she eased back and brushed light fingers along his jaw. 'I love you,' she declared gently.

He released his seatbelt. 'Let's go inside, hmm?'

The large double doors swung open as they emerged from the car and Lily came down the few steps to greet them.

Lianne caught her mother close in a hug. 'You were in on this?'

'Isn't it a lovely surprise?'

They entered the foyer, and Lianne stopped in her tracks. 'The furniture.' She turned towards Tyler. 'It's the same…' A lump rose in her throat. He must have persuaded the previous owners to sell a few pieces.

'I purchased it all.'

Her eyes widened. 'Everything?'

'Everything,' he assured solemnly, and he gave a husky laugh as she launched herself into his arms.

Minutes later he gently disentangled her arms from around his neck and eased his mouth from hers. 'I have a feeling we might be embarrassing your mother.'

'Later,' Lianne promised softly.

Tyler lifted a hand and brushed gentle fingers over her mouth. 'There's just one more thing.'

'You mean there's *more*?'

His lips curved into a warm smile. 'Sharon and Zoe are waiting for you and Lily upstairs.'

She could drown in the depths of those dark eyes. 'Why?'

'To help you change and get ready.'

'Get ready for what?' She was paraphrasing his words, but she couldn't help herself.

'A reaffirmation of our wedding vows.'

An entire gamut of emotions passed fleetingly across her expressive features. 'You're kidding... aren't you?' she asked in a voice little above a whisper.

'I've never been more serious in my life.'

Dear Lord in heaven. 'I don't have any clothes with me.'

'There's a complete outfit upstairs.' He touched a light finger to the tip of her nose. 'Go.'

Lianne turned towards her mother. 'You knew and you didn't tell me?'

Lily smiled and lifted both hands in defence. 'I was sworn to secrecy.'

'All of you?'

'Darling,' Lily chided as she took her daughter's arm. 'You're wasting time.'

Together they ascended the wide curving staircase and made their way to the main bedroom.

'Unbelievable,' Lianne reiterated, as she took in the exquisite furnishings, the furniture...everything was exactly as it had been the day she'd viewed it with Tyler.

If the gesture overwhelmed her, the thought of re-affirming their wedding vows blew her away.

Sharon and Zoe took turns in enveloping Lianne in a hug as soon as she stepped into the main bedroom. 'OK,' Sharon directed with a warm smile. 'Let's get this show on the road.' She checked her watch. 'Fifty minutes and counting.'

Lianne was ready with five minutes to spare. After taking the quickest shower on record, she slipped into lingerie, added an exquisite gown in ivory satin-edged silk chiffon and scalloped lace. Make-up was kept to a minimum, with emphasis on her eyes, and pink gloss colouring her lips. Her hair was swept into a careless twist and Sharon added a few strategically placed single crystal-bead clips. Next came a diamond pendant, matching ear-studs and bracelet.

A touch of perfume, then Lily, Sharon and Zoe stood back to admire their handiwork.

'Thanks.' Lianne hugged each of them. 'You're the best.'

'Almost forgot,' Sharon exclaimed as she crossed to the bed, caught up a single ivory rose and placed it in Lianne's hand.

They walked to the head of the staircase and Lianne stood for a few seconds as she took in the scene below.

The spacious foyer held a small round table directly beneath the crystal chandelier, and three dark-suited men stood grouped together with a neatly attired grey-haired matron.

Tyler raised his head and Lianne felt her bones begin to melt as his mouth curved into a warm smile, just for her. It was if his soul merged with her own and everything faded from her vision.

There was only him, a recognition of the depth of his love…and the joy of knowing nothing, *nothing*, could ever come between them again. Whatever the future held, they were in it together.

Her answering smile held a radiance that tugged at his heart and sent it into a heavy beat. She was beautiful, inside and out, and the love of his life.

Lianne began descending the stairs and Tyler walked slowly to meet her. When she reached the final step he held out his hand and she placed her own on to his palm, felt his fingers close over hers, only to have the breath hitch in her throat as he lifted her hand to his lips.

His eyes were dark and so impossibly deep she could almost drown in them. Her mouth shook a little and he lifted his free hand to brush light fingers over the soft, tremulous curve.

'If you cry I'm going to have to kiss you,' he teased gently.

The faint shimmering moistness acquired a sparkle. 'And shock the celebrant?'

Tyler's eyes gleamed. 'Everyone is waiting.'

It was a touching ceremony, brief, but meaningful, and Lianne looked in surprise as Tyler slid her wedding ring in place, followed it with her engagement ring, both of which she'd torn off almost five months ago. Then he added a magnificent diamond-studded band.

'Eternity.'

Now she really was going to cry.

His mouth closed over hers in a lingering kiss that took hold of her senses and sent them soaring.

This, *this* was the happiest moment of her life, and she told him so. All the pain, the heartbreak, had dissolved and disappeared. In its place was love. The deep abiding kind.

'You're my life,' Tyler said gently. 'My love. Everything.'

It was Chris who broke open the champagne, Clive who made a toast to their future, and Lily who announced her love for them all.

The celebrant left at dusk. Lily and Sharon produced sufficient food for a banquet, and followed it with a small, beautifully iced cake.

There was more champagne, much happiness and laughter, and it was after nine when her parents, Chris and Sharon declared their intention to leave.

Shantel had been the perfect babe, sleeping in between feeds, then promptly settling again.

Zoe offered yet another hug and said quietly close to Lianne's ear, 'I'm so happy for you.'

Lianne stood with Tyler in the open doorway as the two cars eased towards the gates, and when the last set of tail-lights disappeared from view they closed the door and she turned and wrapped her arms round Tyler's waist.

He'd discarded his jacket, removed his tie and unbuttoned the top buttons of his shirt. He felt warm, strong and wonderful.

Warmth flooded through her veins and her pulse

picked up its beat at the thought of how the night would end.

'I guess we should leave too.'

He pressed his lips to her hair. 'We're not going anywhere.'

'We're not?'

His eyes were incredibly warm. 'No.'

She lifted her arms and wound them round his neck. 'OK.'

Tyler lowered his head and brushed her lips with his own. 'Easy to please, hmm?'

'All I need is you,' Lianne said gently and met his hungry mouth with a passion that dispensed everything except the sensual magic they shared.

Piercing sweetness arrowed through her body as she absorbed his leashed strength and sought to test it.

With a single fluid movement he swept her into his arms and ascended the stairs. She eased his shirt aside and buried her mouth against warm skin, nipped, and felt the reaction of his body.

'You want to make it to the bedroom?' Tyler groaned close to her ear, and she trailed gentle fingers over his mouth.

She cast him an innocent look. 'You want me to stop?'

He merely quickened his pace, and let her slide down to her feet when he reached the bed.

'My dress—'

His fingers reached for the zip fastening, carefully lowering it until she could step out of it. The killer heels went while he removed each of the pins from her hair.

They took their time until the last vestige of clothing was removed, enjoying the anticipation, the myriad sensations that built until they could no longer be denied.

In one easy movement Tyler leant forward and tossed back the bedcovers, then he drew her down on to the bed, his kisses so hot, his hands so incredibly sensual as they slid over her skin in an erotic exploration that drove her wild.

Their lovemaking became a feasting of the senses, a pleasure trove that transcended anything they'd previously shared. A meshing of mind, body and soul they were both reluctant to have end.

Afterwards they lay together, sated in a post coital euphoria that had no need for words, then they showered and returned to bed.

Lianne drifted into a dreamless sleep and came slowly awake some time through the night to the slow glide of Tyler's hand as it shaped her hip then slid down to her thigh and lingered there.

He sensed the change in her breathing, the quickened pulse-beat, and he stretched out and switched on the bedlamp, wanting, needing to see her as he sought her mouth with his own, savouring in a sensual exploration that melted her bones.

It was a while before he raised his head and she almost died at the wealth of emotion evident in his dark eyes. Everything he felt for her was there, laid bare, and it was almost too much.

He watched those glorious sapphire-blue depths shimmer then well as one tear spilled and slid slowly across her temple and disappeared into her hair.

'I love you,' Tyler vowed gently. 'More than life itself.'

'Same goes.' Her voice was little more than a tremulous heartfelt whisper. There was one thing she needed to say. 'You have my trust. Always.'

They were words from the heart, which he would forever treasure. 'Thank you,' he accepted simply, aware of what it took for her to gift them to him. 'Believe you will never have cause for doubt.'

'I know,' Lianne said quietly, reaching for him, wanting, needing to show him he held her heart, her soul.

Maybe soon there would be a child. She fervently hoped so. It would be the ultimate gift.

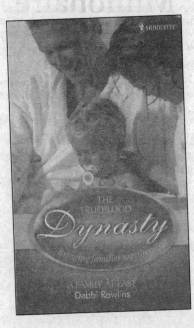

4 FREE

BOOKS AND A SURPRISE GIFT!

We would like to take this opportunity to thank you for reading this Mills & Boon® book by offering you the chance to take FOUR more specially selected titles from the Modern Romance™ series absolutely FREE! We're also making this offer to introduce you to the benefits of the Reader Service™—

- ★ FREE home delivery
- ★ FREE gifts and competitions
- ★ FREE monthly Newsletter
- ★ Exclusive Reader Service offers
- ★ Books available before they're in the shops

Accepting these FREE books and gift places you under no obligation to buy, you may cancel at any time, even after receiving your free shipment. Simply complete your details below and return the entire page to the address below. You don't even need a stamp!

YES! Please send me 4 free Modern Romance books and a surprise gift. I understand that unless you hear from me, I will receive 6 superb new titles every month for just £2.75 each, postage and packing free. I am under no obligation to purchase any books and may cancel my subscription at any time. The free books and gift will be mine to keep in any case.

P5ZED

Ms/Mrs/Miss/Mr ....Initials ....
BLOCK CAPITALS PLEASE

Surname ....

Address ....

....

.................................Postcode.................................

Send this whole page to:
UK: FREEPOST CN81, Croydon, CR9 3WZ